UNLIKELY STORIES

Fatal Fantasies and Delusions

*I dedicate this book to
my wife, Carol*

Contents

Las Vegas Confession

F... it. I don't care anymore. Whatever happened—dream or reality—had to happen. Who gives a damn? Afterwards, it all feels the same, like a distant memory, something remote and small and diminished...a world glimpsed through the wrong end of a telescope. Like this woman, this girl in Vegas, the one who...well, she was a dwarf, a midget of some kind.... Believe me.

No, no, no. I'm sorry. I shouldn't say this. In polite society, we don't use words like that. We use softer terms. Cripples are 'Physically Challenged.' Retards are 'Mentally Challenged.' Right? And dwarfs are to be called 'Little People.'

But, sometimes, I'm not so smooth. I tend to say the unsayable, utter the unutterable.

She worked in one of those gambling joints where they have live circus acts: trapeze artistes, jugglers, fire-eaters, jumping poodles, clowns. But I'm getting ahead of myself as always, helter-skelter, without plan or preamble.

A lot happened on that trip, that I'm not too clear about. Las Vegas started sapping my mental powers soon after I got there. And with each passing hour, my thinking got fuzzier and fuzzier. In fact, this process started even before I landed. Believe me.

My plane banks over the city, well past midnight, and slopes towards the runway. I peer out of the oval window at the black emptiness streaming past. I don't see anything, except my reflection in the plexiglass—a haggard mask I do not recognize, wish to disown. The scotch 'n' sodas I downed earlier have all but worn off and my mouth feels like it's full of copper pennies. I need another drink, but the seat belt sign comes on and soon afterwards a river of lights appears below us, glittering and twinkling like diamonds and rubies and emeralds scattered on black velvet. The galactic razzle-dazzle raises my spirits even though I really don't want to be here. Believe me.

I get off the plane and hurry to a bar in the airport lounge to fortify my nerves before I face the luggage carrousel. The slow, circular movement of suitcases and garment bags makes me suicidal. Post-flight let-down, I guess. Also, Vegas can be intimidating. The city's dealt lousy hands to many and sent 'em home broke, babbling.

I'm here for a computer trade show, along with hundreds of others. I spot the various types milling around in the Baggage Claim area. The veeps are in dark, wrinkled suits, middle-managers are wearing striped shirts and loud neckties and the programmers have on jeans, jogging shoes and T-shirts covered with logos and slogans. Nearly all the programmers have pot-bellies and scraggy beards. The mid-level guys sport trimmed mustaches and the veeps are all clean-shaven.

This is not a group I wish to spend too much time with. They can talk of nothing but bits and bytes and sales channels.

I do have to meet a few people that my company has sent me here to see. The rest of the time, I plan on staying pleasantly numb by maintaining a certain level of alcohol in my bloodstream. If I do all this adroitly, the entire trip should be a painless, rosy blur. I won't even remember having been here when I get back to California. That, at least, is my plan. Believe me.

In the lobby of my hotel, the racket of gambling machines assaults my senses. There are scores of different types lined up in neat rows like soldiers of a robotic army. Lights blink, bells clang, levers come down: KA-CHUNG! KARA-CHUNG! and the clatter of coins hitting tin trays makes the air shiver.

I will not gamble, I say to myself. It seems stupid to me, stupid and unamusing. But I'm not a Puritan.

If I'm going to spend money, it might as well be on some sweet-young-thing who'll do lewd and lascivious things to me. Or I could find a good restaurant and have a memorable meal. Whatever...

I enter my room, deposit my bags, freshen up, and take the elevator back to the lobby. By all calculations, I should be sleepy, but for some reason, I'm not. A zany, manic energy surges through me, making my muscles ache. It's almost two in the morning and the lobby is full of gamblers. Waitresses in micro-mini skirts and black mesh stockings carry drinks to the patrons in hopes of keeping them mellowed out so they'll quit worrying about losing money. The waitresses have baggy-eyed, middle-aged faces but nifty legs. I suppose, when they get too old for the chorus line and all the bump 'n' grind shows in town, they wait on tables. *C'est la vie a la Vegas.*

The noise and the lights prove bothersome, so I head for a bar in a quiet corner and buy a cognac. I drink it quickly and get another one. But before I can finish the second drink, it feels as though the lights are getting dim. I've got about five minutes to get to my room before the curtain falls. I ooze off my stool unsteadily and lurch towards the elevator on rubbery legs. I don't even remember opening the door of my room much less falling on the bed fully clothed. Believe me.

The trade-show proves to be a prolonged migraine. I wander through the long aisles like a lost soul looking for salvation. Starry-eyed pitch-men try to get my attention with terrific bargains and state-of-the-art, leading-edge technology. But I'm immune to their temptations because I've maxed out my credit card. The deals I'm looking for have to be made for the people who sent me here. I spend the day tracking down my contacts and hash out the fine-print in lengthy contracts. Later that night, after a bloody meal of rare steak and heavy red wine, I find myself alone and footloose. I go prowling through the gaudy, gilded casinos, looking for trouble. I feel strangely aggressive, like a black panther in the jungles of Amazonia...a Bengal tiger loping through lush carpeting and luxuriant growths of cocktail-waitress...a mafia hit-man on a mission to rub out a rival boss...a secret agent on the tail of a Russian spy with big boobs and secrets to sell. I want to do something daring—dangerous...

Psychiatrists have a name for this illness, but one doesn't own up to it in polite society. Believe me.

So...I stop at a vending machine and buy a pack of chewing gum. There are messages and phone numbers pasted on the machine. 'For a good time call 777-2148.' Do I want a good time? Or do I want to sit down somewhere and rest my aching feet?

Bored by the scene in the tawdry lobby, I step out to the street to catch a cab. But just as I fall into the back seat and start to give directions to the driver, the door of the cab opens suddenly and an old harpy in a purple wig sticks her head in.

'Mind if we share a cab, sonny?' she says with a loopy grin.

I stare at her, wondering what I should do. Damn my luck! She's obviously had a few. Her lipstick's smeared all over her mouth and the mascara smudged around her eyes makes her look like a raccoon.

Why couldn't she have been the double agent from Moscow, the one with big tits?

Before I can say a word, the hag tumbles in, slams the door shut and flashes her dentures at me.

'Thanks,' she says. 'One can't get a damn cab since the convention's been in town.

'Where are you going?' I ask.

'Nowhere,' she says. 'I mean, nowhere in particular. I'll go wherever you're going.'

'Uhuh,' I stutter. 'I'm going to Garvey's.'

'Garvey's sounds fine, sonny. Let's go to Garvey's. I just won two thousand dollars and something tells me I'm going to win much more before the sun comes up.'

All of a sudden, I don't feel so hostile towards her. She's just another tourist, I figure, being suckered by the system.

'You better leave town before you lose everything you've won,' I tell her.

'Naa aah,' she says. 'I don't mind losing. Moreover, I live here.'

This shuts me up and I sit silently as the cab takes us to Garvey's. When we get there, I pay the driver and we step out.

'Come,' says the old bag, 'You look like a nice guy. I'll buy you a drink.'

'A deal,' I tell her and we head for the bar.

'So you live here?' I say. 'I guess it makes sense. But I just can't imagine anyone actually living in this town. The whole place is so much like a stage show. I get the feeling that all the people—the workers, are just actors who take off their uniforms at dawn and vanish into thin air.'

She orders a gin and tonic and I get myself a scotch-on-the-rocks.

'Well, very few people actually live in town,' she says. 'I have a trailer-home parked on a few acres about fifteen miles out of town.'

'That makes sense,' I say.

'My daughter works at the Circus Casino,' she adds. 'I moved here to be close to her.'

'Your daughter?'

'Yup,' she says and lights a cigarette. 'In fact, she'll be getting off in a few hours and I have to pick her up.'

'What does she do at the Circus?' I ask.

'Oh, a bunch of stuff,' says the old lady. 'She's got a great act, mostly on the tight rope. That girl can balance on a dime. This is a mother's biased opinion, I know, but she really is pretty good. She wouldn't have survived in the biz otherwise.'

'I can imagine,' I murmur.

We sip our drinks in silence for a while as she finishes her cigarette.

'So you're with the convention?' she says.

I nod.

'I thought so,' she says.

'How can you tell?'

'All you computer guys look like zombies,' she says.

'That's a rather drastic generalization,' I counter.

'I know,' she says, grinning and stubs out her cigarette.

'Look,' sonny,' she adds. 'I'm going to gamble some more.
You wanna join me or you wanna sit here and get pickled?'

'I'll watch,' I say. 'I want to learn your winning system.'

She throws back her head and laughs.

'Come along,' she says. 'I'll show you my system.'

So I get off my stool and follow her.

Believe me.

For the next couple of hours I watched her go from one
slot machine to the next, pulling levers, pushing buttons,
banging on the glass-faces of ungenerous one-armed bandits.
From the slots she went to the black-jack tables, roulette,
craps, lucky 7, poker, and every other wagering station. She'd
win ten and lose fifteen, or she'd win a hundred and lose
two hundred. But in general the trend was down. It took
her a couple of hours to lose the two thousand dollars, but
by three in the morning she'd been picked clean like the
carcass of a Wildebeeste left out on the Serengeti.

'This is my last quarter,' she said finally, shoving a coin
into a slot-machine.

When no cheerful rain of coins fell into the tray below,
she announced: 'Now I'm broke.'

'Sorry,' I said. 'I thought you had a winning system.'

'I do,' she said, 'but tonight I'm out of time and money.
I've got to pick up my girl. In fact, why don't you come
along. We can go out to my trailer and I'll cook us all a big
breakfast.'

I thought for a moment. It sounded like a wacky plan,
but I was in a wacky mood and didn't have much else to do.

'Okay,' I said, 'let's go.'

'We'll have to get a cab,' she said.

'You don't have a car?' I said, a hint of incredulity in my tone.

'Naaaah,' she said. 'Lost my licence years ago—kept running into things—and my daughter can't drive.'

'Uh-huh,' I said.

We stepped out of Garvey's and hailed a cab.

'The Circus,' she told the driver. 'Stage entrance.'

'Yes, ma'am,' said the driver, smacking his gum loudly. 'Anything you say.'

The cab moved off the neon-bright main drag and entered a region of dark, back alleys cluttered with garbage cans and empty cardboard boxes. We drove past hulking sheds and warehouses with roll-up steel doors and concrete loading ramps in front. It all looked like the set of a B-grade gangster flick. Believe me.

Eventually, we came up to large hangar-like structure with a massive gate that rolled on wheels as big as those on a Volkswagen. In the deathly white light of arc lamps, I saw a six or seven digit number painted on it in foot tall numerals.

I rolled down my window and a sharp, acrid odor clawed my sinuses. Urine, I thought. All those circus animals — zebras, lions, tigers, chimps—had really pissed up the place. Then I heard the off-key trumpeting of an elephant, lamenting the loss of his mother, Africa. Believe me.

'Honk your horn,' said the old witch to the driver. 'She'll come out when she hears you.'

The cabby tapped out the opening notes of a Beethoven symphony.

A small, side door swung open, spilling a ribbon of orange light and a little girl all bundled up in lacy shawls and silken wraps came running towards us. I barely caught the quick-flash glimmer of pink satin slippers, when the front door of the cab opened and a wave of silk and sequins crashed in, scattering molecules of some rich, musky perfume.

'Where to?' the cabby asked.

'North Vegas, honey,' the old woman said. 'Take the highway. I'm about fifteen miles from town. I'll tell you when we get close to the off ramp.'

'Hi, Mom,' said the girl, turning her head to look at us. 'Who's this?'

The voice shocked me. I expected the shrill, piping tones of a child. Instead, I heard the deep, resonant voice of a mature woman.

A midget, I thought. Oh, my god, she's a midget!

'An old friend, sweetie,' said the old lady. 'I ran into him by chance. What was your name, hon?'

'Jay,' I said.

'Jay,' said the little person. 'I'm Tina but everyone calls me Princess Zanzanna.'

'You sound tired, dear,' her mother said. 'Did you have a good time tonight?'

'Fine. Well…no actually, one of the elephants tried to eat my wig.'

'Really? The one you're wearing? How did that happen?'

'He snatched it off my head and started to stuff it into his mouth.'

'Oh god. Now we'll have to buy a new one.'

'No, no, The trainer got him to spit it out. I don't think the elephant really cared much for the taste of synthetic hair.'

She chuckled.

I just sat there quietly, listening to them talk. The wig in question was rather a grand object, curled and coiled elaborately like the extravagant creations worn by Dolly Parton.

After a longish drive, we finally pulled up in front of their mobile home. We'd left the glitter and glitz of the Strip far behind and were in a region of bare, unpopulated desert. We piled out of the taxi in front of their trailer home and I paid the driver. He turned his vehicle around smartly and took off, spraying gravel in our faces.

Their mobile home sat all by itself in a patch of beige-colored sand and all around us stretched the vast expanse of the desert, glowing softly under the faint star-light. And far away on the eastern horizon, one could see the silhouettes of distant hills, inky black against the backdrop of a purple sky.

The trailer proved to be surprisingly spacious. Perhaps they had a double wide—two units bolted together. I didn't ask. I went and sat in the living room and waited for breakfast to be served. Tina plopped down beside me, with her feet up.

Tina made me feel a bit awkward and I wondered how she expected to be treated: like a little girl or a grown woman?

'God, my feet hurt,' she said suddenly and made a face. 'Look how the wire rope cuts into them.'

She removed her slippers and placed her feet in my lap. This impulsive but utterly innocent gesture made me suck in my breath.

I looked down and saw the deep grooves left by the ropes on the soles of her feet.

'You poor thing,' I said and started to rub her feet gently. 'I bet they hurt.'

'Oooo, that feels good,' she cooed. 'You can keep doing that.'

Her feet felt soft and small in my hands and as I massaged them, a genuine sense of sympathy swept over me. I wished she didn't have to earn her living getting crucified every night on the high wire.

Meanwhile, Mildred got going in the kitchen. Swiftly she pulled out what she needed from the refrigerator and various other kitchen cabinets and was soon cracking eggs with practised dexterity.

'I make the best darn huevos rancheros west of the Pecos,' she said.

'I'll be the judge of that,' I snapped back with mock sternness.

She giggled and then said: 'Fine. But first why don't you crack open some champagne to wake up your taste buds. I think there is a bottle in the ice-box.'

As I got up to do the honors, Tina also rose.

'I'm going to take a shower and change into something comfortable,' she said. 'I can't eat right after I get off work. I'm all wound up tight like spring.'

'Go right ahead honey,' her mother said. 'It'll take me a while to get the food up.'

I turned my attention to the fridge and discovered not one but over half a dozen magnums of champagne in there. I grabbed one and set about pulling out the cork.

'Here are some glasses,' said the old lady and set three crystal champagne flutes on the kitchen counter.

'There's one thing I insist on,' she went on, as she hacked up an onion with deft ferocity. 'One must drink out of a glass that is appropriate for the liquor.'

'Damn right,' I said, as I eased the cork up carefully, working it upward with the pressure of opposing thumbs. It came out with a soft POP and a froth of white bubbles rose to the bottle's mouth. I poured the wine into the tall tulip-shaped glasses carefully and every time the creamy foam rose to the brim and threatened to flow over the side, I'd wait until it settled down.

'Here,' I said, handing a glass to the old lady. 'What should we toast?'

She frowned as she took the glass from me and shook her head.

'No,' she said. 'This wine is too good to be mixed with emotions.'

'I see your point. Why run the risk of spoiling the taste?'

'Exactly.'

The champagne proved to be crisp and dry. It danced on the palate like a rain of sparks struck from an iceberg and made my brain cells tingle.

'This is excellent stuff,' I said. 'I don't think I've ever had better bubbly.'

'I buy it by the case,' said the old lady. 'That way I get it for much less than you'd pay for worse stuff at your local liquor store.'

I emptied my glass rather quickly and then poured myself some more.

The old lady turned her attention to the eggs once again and hurried them along.

'Why don't you set the table,' she suggested. 'The dishes are over there in that cabinet next to the refrigerator.'

I put down my glass and did as I was told.

I was on my third glass of champagne when Princess Zanzanna emerged from her room. She had taken off the bizarre wig and removed the heavy, stage make-up. She looked so different—much younger and more innocent—that I almost didn't recognize her. I was tempted to stare at her, but tried hard not to. She was even prettier without all that make-up. Her own hair was dark reddish-brown and cut very short like a boy's. She had wrapped a silky red robe around herself and I got the distinct impression that underneath the robe she wasn't wearing anything.

'Have some champagne,' I said. 'Before it goes flat.'

'Don't mind if I do,' she said. 'That shower felt good.'

'This'll make you feel even better,' I said handing her a brimming glass.

The kitchen counter was about as high as Tina's chin, but apart from being short she was perfectly formed.

She had a charming smile, warm, brown eyes, and a narrow waist. Her hands and feet were dainty and—what surprised me most—she possessed a pair of fairly voluptuous breasts that any full-size teen-age beauty queen would have been proud to own.

'Would you please do my feet again?' she said to me, flopping down on the couch, champagne glass in hand. 'You have an excellent touch.'

'With pleasure,' I said gallantly, kneeling down beside the couch.

Presently, the air became fragrant with the odor of fried onions, eggs and sausage and the old lady brought the food to the table and we sat down to eat. Tina sat on her own special high chair that had, no doubt, been built for her.

'You were right,' I told the old lady. 'These are the best huevos rancheros I've ever had.'

She smiled and said: 'Have some more. Don't be shy.'

I don't remember much more about what was said as we ate. But I do recall that I kept going to the refrigerator and pulling out bottles of champagne. I think I must have opened four or five or, maybe, even six. I don't know. At some point, I stopped counting.

Eventually my head turned into one giant, glowing bubble floating serenely on a golden sea of champagne. And during the course of the meal, I remember thinking that I'd never met anyone as charming as Tina or her mother and that I'd never had as nice a time drinking and eating with anyone as I was having with those two.

The sun had cleared the eastern horizon by the time the party broke up. Everyone seemed agreed to call it a night. Mildred helped me up from the chair and pointed me towards the guest bedroom.

'That way, buster. There's a bed in there for you.'

'Great breakfast,' I said to her. 'Thanks.' I bowed in an elaborate Old World way and went off singing 'Good-night, Irene, Good night.'

Sodden with champagne as I was, I think I barely had enough strength to take off my clothes before collapsing on the bed. After that—oblivion.

And then all of a sudden, I'm in this dream, it seems, and I'm wide awake and very alert..Believe me.

I open my eyes but I can't see a thing. The darkness in the room is thick and impenetrable like the darkness inside a tomb. I'm breathing hard like a panting dog, my breath coming and going in ragged gasps. Where am I? I wonder, straining my ears to pick up some sounds or noises. At first the silence all around is heavy and seamless. But then I hear someone whispering my name.

'Who?' I mumble. 'Who?' I'm trying to unstick my tongue from the roof of my mouth.

'Shhhhh,' comes the response. 'It's me.'

I recognize the voice instantly and then I feel small hands and gentle fingers racing lightly over my legs.

This has got to be a dream, I say to myself. This can't be happening.

But there are lips close to my ears now, murmuring something. And a rich, musky odor swirls around my head.

I reach out and touch her head and my palms rub up against short, close-cropped hair. It feels soft and springy. I run my hand down to her neck and along her shoulders and my fingers come into contact with the cool, silken fabric of her robe. I wait for her to say something but she doesn't utter a sound. I put an arm around her and scoop her up into bed with me. The robe falls away and I feel the cool, softness of her full breasts against my face. I turn and kiss her cheeks and eyes. She clings to me, her chest pressed up tightly against mine and moans.

'It's okay,' I tell her. 'It's okay.'

Her cheeks feel wet, as if she's been crying. I wipe away her tears and kiss her on the mouth. Her lips part and I feel her tongue flutter against mine.

Then she unwraps her arms from around my neck and slides down along my body, planting little kisses as she goes. She pulls and tugs at the elastic waistband of my underwear. I assist her in getting the shorts off and feel myself rising up to meet her mouth.

By now my brain has shut off completely and I find that I'm on some kind of pre-programmed sexual auto-pilot. I pull her up and kiss her fiercely, letting my hands rove across her hills and valleys and chasms. She feels supple and strong. Her arms and legs are lean and muscular, like those of a gymnast. I sense a tremendous strength in her limbs, but also a great flexibility. She bends, twists and turns as though she didn't have a single bone in her body.

At some point, she sits on top of me and starts to move up and down as though she were riding a horse. I encircle her narrow waist with both hands to help her and to make sure she doesn't fall off.

And then I open all her files, explore every nook and cranny of her database. My fingers go tap, tap, tapping on her keyboard, trying to read the code on her secret sectors. I look at all her tracks and take note of her configuration. I nibble her bits and take big greedy bytes out of her floppy disks. She gasps with shock and responds by tickling my peripherals. I look for her sockets and stroke them with my tongue until voltage arcs from her flesh to mine. And even in the blinding darkness that engulfs us, I can see we are totally compatible. Her nodes talk to my nodes in perfect synchrony. And when she finally spreads her spreadsheet before me, so tragically small and vulnerable, all I can do is enter and let the microchips fall where they might.

Believe me.

Then I wake up and I'm all alone.

I can't remember where I am. I stumble to a window and pull a curtain aside. The sun is setting in a halo of fire and brimstone and a beam of orange light probes the room like an accusatory finger. My head throbs like a pus-filled pimple.

I drag on my clothes and step out of the room. The kitchen and the dining nook have been cleaned up and all the dishes washed and put away. The place is neat as a pin.

'Hullo,' I croak. 'Anyone home?'

But there is no answer. My eyes fall on a yellow stick-note on the countertop. There is only one word on it written with a thick black felt, pen: 'LATER.'

What followed, need not be documented—the expensive cab ride back to town, the liquored-up flight home and the hangover that lingered for days on end. But...you know that story already. Believe me.

The Laid-Off Man

Dev woke with a start and squinted bleary-eyed at the digital clock-radio on the bedside table. In the early-morning dark, glowing red numbers announced the time with pitiless precision: 5:55. As always, he'd woken up exactly five minutes ahead of the alarm. Alongside him on the double bed, Rushmi still slept soundly.

Then it occurred to him—he didn't have to worry about the alarm going off. He hadn't set it the night before. He was a laid-off man. He didn't have to get up early anymore. A laid-off person has no job to go to, no need to get up, get dressed, swallow soggy corn-flakes and rush off to work.

He shut his eyes tightly, grimly determined to not think about being unemployed. If he could only sleep a little longer....But he couldn't. His heart had started to thump like a runaway drum solo and his brain was replaying every painful moment of his last day at Techware Solutions.

Techware hadn't been doing well for a long time. This much, everyone knew. In fact, all the local newspapers had been running stories for months on the 'meteoric' rise and slow decline of Techware. The editors who tracked high-tech companies were quick to assign blame. Some said it was the fault of the management; others, the weak economy. Still others felt that Techware's products were out-of-date and lacked the nifty features offered by competitors for much less money. And then there were those who blamed Japan. In fact, blaming the Japanese had become very popular all over the country. As jobs vanished and the lines of the unemployed got longer and longer, everyone wanted a scapegoat.

For over six months Dev had been hearing rumors about a massive lay-off. But he didn't think Techware would fire him. Hell, he had seniority; he'd been with the company for over five years. Moreover, he'd been working on a high-priority project for nearly eighteen months. He was the only one who could wrap it up. He felt, more or less, secure.

But then everything changed one sunny day. Techware started chopping heads and Dev found himself among the casualties. Dozens of other employees also were forced to clean out desks and evacuate their cubicles. There were quick, embarrassed handshakes and farewell hugs on every floor. Tears in the parking-lot. Promises were made to stay in touch. Some left stoically silent. Others bitched about 'unfair tactics,' 'capitalism in action,' even 'blatant racism.' Before all the blood-letting came to a halt, even engineers who'd been with the company for over ten years found themselves pink-slipped and put out to pasture.

Dev blamed himself for this sudden reversal in his fortunes. Feeling guilty came naturally to him. His ethnic background and family influences had molded him to always consider his own deficiencies when faced with failure, rejection and unsuccess. He must have some inherent flaw or shortcoming in his character, he reasoned. He must have done something wrong, or displeased his managers in some way. He must not have performed to the high standards that Techware espoused as a company. He must not have worked hard enough or fast enough. Perhaps he hadn't put in extra time at his computer. Or, (and this charge hurt most of all) he simply didn't have the smarts to be a Techware employee.

However, Bob Wilson, (another victim of the lay-off) refused to take the blame for Techware's decline.

'Look, man, we got lousy leadership,' Bob told Dev on the phone. 'We did exactly what they told us to do, but they never came up with a good strategy. Short-sighted planning and plain old greed, that's what got us into trouble. Instead of taking some of those earnings—all the bucks they made in the early years—and plowing them into research and development, the top managers simply skimmed the profits and made themselves rich.'

'O well,' Dev sighed. 'Maybe we didn't work hard enough.'

'Shit, I gained one hundred pounds from sitting at the computer for all those hours,' Bob said. 'Don't tell me I didn't work hard enough.'

'I know. I know you did,' Dev responded.

'Techware was robbed from the inside, my man,' Bob said. 'Plundered and mismanaged.'

'Well, I suppose you're right,' Dev murmured. 'But what can one do? We're just cogs caught in a bigger machine.'

'The hell we are,' Bob said with real energy. 'I'm not taking this lying down.'

'But ...'

'I'm going to get even with these bastards. They can't use me and throw me aside like, like I'm some kind of garbage.'

'Take it easy, Bob,' Dev advised. 'Calm down. You'll find another job. Surely.'

Bob did have a point. Several of the top people had transformed themselves from ordinary, middle-class types into multi-millionaires in just a few years. The president and his chosen gang of vice presidents bought thousands of shares of company stock at a penny-a-share and sold it at over $50 a share. They made honey-sweet, barely legal, inside deals and awarded generous bonuses and dividends to themselves. But even as this gang of four or five got rich, Techware, as a company, dwindled and declined and slowly melted away like a popsicle on a hot side walk.

* * *

Growing weary of tossing and turning and afraid of waking up his wife, Dev got up and headed for the kitchen. Rushmi needed her sleep. She worked long hours as a clerk at a nearby grocery store. They'd been married for a little over two years and only recently had she begun to feel secure enough to start talking about having a baby He got along well with her, even though he hadn't known her before they'd tied the knot. Theirs had been an arranged marriage. Dev's parents had selected Rushmi and planned everything according to the customs of the Brahmin families of Rameshwaram, the little South Indian village where he'd grown up.

His American friends couldn't understand how he could have married a girl he'd never dated. They often teased him about marrying a complete stranger. But he'd smile politely and point out the high failure rate among typical All-American love-matches.

'You'd think these love-marriages which start so wonderfully, I mean, all the dating, etcetera—you'd think they'd last. But they don't,' he said defensively. 'Arranged marriages work well for our people. It's a matter of customs and traditions.'

'Hey, can you get me a mail-order bride?' Bob Wilson kidded him. 'Is there a catalog or something—with pictures? I mean, how do you know which one to send for?'

'What if you end up with someone you just can't stand,' Ron Henchard wanted to know. 'Can you return the merchandise and get your money back?'

Dev did his best to explain how matches were made in India. He took pains to describe all the social nuances which governed the establishment of matrimonial alliances, all the delicate diplomacy and negotiations that went on between two families of equal social rank and similar cultural backgrounds. But his colleagues simply rolled their eyes and grinned and smirked. They had no interest in the traditions of India. The American way of doing everything was the best way. Right?

* * *

Dev made a pot of tea, (another cultural habit he had not been able to let go) and started looking over the morning paper. There might be an opening somewhere. Another

company might be looking for a software engineer. Even
though jobs had been few and far between lately, like a
trained rat he went through the ritual of looking every single
day.

Suddenly, the name of his old company caught his eye.
'Disturbance at Techware,' read the headline and the sub-
head gave a few more details: 'Disgruntled Ex-Employee
Terrorizes Workers.'

Dev put down his cup and quickly scanned the story. 'A
disgruntled, ex-employee created a major disturbance at
Techware Solutions on Friday afternoon. The company,
which develops software, found itself under a virtual siege as
the man roamed the corridors of the building, shouting
insults and making threatening gestures. Responding to a
911 call, a SWAT team evacuated the building and arrested
the man. The intruder, one Bob Wilson, apparently upset
over being laid-off, decided to vent his frustration in a public
display of anger. He was unarmed but appeared to be
intoxicated. "We're seeing lots of similar incidents lately,"
Detective Sergeant Butkus told our reporter. "With the
downturn in the computer industry and all the lay-offs,
people are under a lot of strain. Some of 'em just can't take
it anymore. They flip-out—simply self-destruct."'

Dev put the paper down. His hands were shaking.

He could hardly believe his eyes. The Bob Wilson he
remembered was a decent fellow, so bright, so witty, so
cool-headed. He was a Computer Science graduate from
MIT, for god's sake, not some wacked-out psycho.

Dev raced to the phone and started punching numbers
feverishly. A couple of calls, and he managed to confirm the
newspaper account. The most reliable source of information
proved to be Janet, Bob's current girlfriend. She sounded
relatively calm for someone whose boyfriend was in jail.

'His parents are bailing him out,' she said. The cops had
charged him with disturbing the peace, unlawful trespass,
resisting arrest, and being in possession of a contraband
substance. They'd found some cocaine on him, she told Dev.

'I can't believe this,' Dev murmured. 'I never knew Bob took drugs.'

'Oh, well,' Janet said 'he's not an addict or anything. I mean, who doesn't like to get high once in a while? Nothing wrong with that.'

'Oh?' said Dev.

* * *

When Rushmi woke up, he showed her the Bob Wilson story.

'The guy's gone crazy,' said Dev. 'I can't believe it. His cubicle used to be right next to mine.'

'I'm worried about you,' said Rushmi. 'Bob has a family here. They'll take care of him. You are alone. What are you planning on doing? We can manage on my salary for a while, but we'll have to sell the new car and cut back on extra expenses.'

'I guess we don't need a second car since I'm not working,' Dev murmured. 'I'll put an ad in the paper. We'll lose a ton of money since we've only owned it for a year, but at least we won't have this expense hanging over our heads every month.'

Rushmi nodded in agreement.

'I really don't understand this lay-off business,' she said. 'My father worked all his life for the Indian Railway. We weren't rich, but I don't think Daddy-ji ever worried about waking up some day and being without a job.'

'Nor did my father,' said Dev. 'Our family has been in the silk and coffee business for generations. Daddy didn't even know the meaning of not working.'

'I just don't understand this system,' Rushmi said. 'But I'm sure you'll find another job. However, when you do find work, I'm not going to let you rush out and buy a new car.'

Dev grinned sheepishly.

'I guess I was overly-optimistic,' he said. 'I had no idea
that this economy is flimsy as a house of cards.'

* * *

After Rushmi left for work, Dev paced around the small
apartment like a nervous gerbil. The TV blared loudly with
giggles and laughter and on-camera psychotherapy sessions.
Under the probing scrutiny of cameras, people seemed eager
to reveal all sorts of amazing secrets about their private
lives. Talk Shows had turned the sacred rite of Confession
into a public show. Voyeurism had become respectable. Not
only had these people had done nasty things to each other,
but then they had this inexplicable itch to get on national
TV and wave their filthy laundry in front of a live audience.

Dev flipped the channels listlessly hoping for some news
about India or some interesting report, but only found more
meaningless chatter and sleepwalking soap operas in which
the actors and actresses looked like embalmed corpses.

Seeking relief from the idiocy on TV, he went into the
guest bedroom, turned on his computer and wrote a letter to
his father. He made some general comments about being in
good health and spirits but he didn't mention the lay-off. His
parents wouldn't understand anyway. People in India looked
upon the United States as some kind of magical Wonderland
or El Dorado, where everyone had money and nothing to
worry about. Besides, the exchange rate between the dollar
and the Indian rupee was so lopsided in favor of the dollar
that his folks couldn't really help him money-wise. They had
plenty of problems of their own to contend with.

Next he fiddled with his résumé, updating it, adding
information, formatting and re-formatting. Then, just for
fun, he decided to write a letter to Meena, his little niece.
He hadn't seen her since her Kindergarten days, but she'd
grown up fast and turned into an articulate young person.
Dev found that communicating with her was like establishing
a link with his own lost childhood. She attended an Irish

Catholic Convent School near Rameshwaram, where the nuns were teaching her English. She had developed into a pretty good letter writer and got a big thrill out of hearing from her 'American' Uncle.

But when he saw the letter he'd written, he grimaced. It looked so dull. The contents were cheerful enough, (he'd described a beach picnic Rushmi had organized a while back) but the printed words *seemed* so boring. 'Wouldn't it be nice if I could actually paint the scene,' he thought, 'really capture the clouds, the ocean, the green grass and the tall, white lighthouse in the background?'

On a whim, he decided to drive over to a nearby art supplies store and get some watercolors and brushes. He would decorate the letter with splashes of color. He wasn't an artist by any stretch, but Meena would enjoy getting a letter filled with colorful illustrations instead of the usual, solid blocks of print he sent her most of the time.

He started to work on his project eagerly as soon as he got back to the apartment. And the more he sketched and painted, the more he wanted to keep at it. He found the process so absorbing that he even forgot about lunch. In fact, he wasn't even aware of being hungry, so enthralled did he become by the magical way in which colors mixed and blended and formed brand new hues as they flowed across the paper.

As the afternoon wore on he realized that a very strange thing had happened. He suddenly found himself perfectly at peace with himself and the world. The nagging anxiety about finding a job, still lingered at the back of his mind, but all the black anger and bitterness that had whipped him up into a frenzy earlier in the day, seemed to have ebbed away.

Time passed imperceptibly. When he looked up from his labors, he was shocked to see that the sun was about to set. It was almost time to set the table and heat the food, pending Rushmi's return.

Dev couldn't remember having spent a more enjoyable day. He was thoroughly hooked on painting, he decided, no doubt about that. He couldn't wait to get paper specially made for watercolors, bigger brushes and more tubes of paint. It had never occurred to him that painting could be so relaxing, so satisfying and so much fun. It did not feel like work, something that fatigued and drained a person, but like a self-replenishing source of pleasure and energy.

Dev had always relished playing with computers and writing programs, but that ultimately proved to be a frustrating and repetitive process. To do well in the profession, you had to keep the frustration in check and go on error-correcting and de-bugging the code until it behaved the way you wanted it to behave. You just had to be very meticulous and stay within a set of prescribed rules of logic and syntax.

But painting with watercolors required an altogether different approach. You did things instinctively, experimentally, unsure of what the end-product would look like. You had to be willing to accept random results, unpredictable consequences. You had to accept the treacherous machinations of gravity, the uncontrollable consequences of water and color mingling on the porous surface of the paper. But all these chance developments and 'happy accidents' were a natural part of the process, a process through which a watercolor painting was not so much created as 'discovered.'

* * *

When Rushmi returned from work, tired and irritable, he proudly showed her the pictures he had painted.

'Very nice, dear,' she said dryly. 'But did you hear from any computer company? Did you send out any more résumés?'

'There is nothing in the paper,' he told her. 'The jobs have simply evaporated.'

'Keep looking, keep trying,' she said patiently. 'You can't just give up.'

'I know, I know,' Dev moaned. 'But all the companies are laying off people. The aeronautics industry is floundering. Semiconductors are sinking. And personal computers are in a real tail-spin.'

'Keep looking, sweetie,' Rushmie responded. 'You're too smart, too highly-trained, too young, to be wasting your life, sitting at home all day watching TV talk shows.'

'I don't want to be sitting at home,' Dev snapped back irritably.

And actually, he didn't. He didn't want to retire at thirty-five, not after spending years and years training and preparing himself to be a computer programmer. He had been the top student at the Computer Engineering department at Berkeley and also back at the Indian Technical Institute. How could he give all that up, just let go of his chosen career as if all his struggles, all that intense mental and physical effort that had gone into training himself—just didn't matter, had no value?

* * *

Over the next few months, Dev kept up his job search. He sent out résumés in response to ads in the paper, called his friends and acquaintances to let them know he wanted a job, and scrutinized the want-ads carefully. But at the same time, he kept on painting.

The painting proved to be a pressure-relief valve for him. He discovered a vast new source of creative energy within himself, an untapped reservoir that he didn't know he possessed. He bought books on art and on watercolors and began to teach himself how to sketch. With every picture he painted, he learned new tricks and techniques. With every picture, he got better and better, more confident of his skills, more knowledgeable about the medium.

As Summer turned into Fall, Dev found out about a Mrs Hammond, an experienced teacher, who gave lessons in watercolor painting. Mrs Hammond held classes in a large workroom behind the Artist's Supplies store where he bought all the paper and paint and brushes he needed. Dev signed up with Mrs Hammond and started attending a class which met on Mondays from 9 to 12. Rather nervous at first, he quickly shed his fears and began to pick up sophisticated techniques that seasoned professionals used.

Once in a while he'd go out on a job interview, but no one made him an offer. These interviews were like getting hit on the head with a sledge hammer. Again and again. You had to be a masochist to keep going through this futile and painful ritual. He got to feeling very discouraged and dispirited. But the joy he derived from his watercolors, kept him moderately sane and cheerful through this grim period of disappointment and rejection. With each passing day he could see improvement in his work. Even Rushmi noticed his progress and kept encouraging him.

Then almost six months into his lessons, his neighbor, Sam Samudio, offered to buy a large painting he'd done of a single yellow rose. Dr Samudio, a dentist by profession, also had a very artistic sensibility plus a love of classical music, expensive cognacs and fine cigars.

'What are you charging for it?' Dr Samudio asked.

'Oh, I don't know,' said Dev. 'I really don't know how much to ask.'

'Well, give me an idea.'

'How about a hundred dollars?'

'It's a deal,' said the good doctor and held out his hand, grinning happily.

Giddy with joy, Dev rushed into the house to tell Rushmi that he'd sold his first painting. Rushmi could hardly trust her ears. She'd heard so many stories of artists starving in garrets, or dying on the streets of Paris, diseased and neglected. She found it hard to believe that anyone could actually make money selling paintings.

* * *

As he got better and better, Dev began to seriously think about trying to make a living as an artist. He started haunting commercial picture galleries and talking to other watercolorists. But he soon realized that none of the artists he met were able to survive on art alone. They did other work to supplement their incomes. But the involvement with art enriched their lives. If he could sell just a few paintings a month, that would do fine. With Rushmi bringing in a small but steady paycheck, they needed just a little bit more to make life comfortable. Later on, as his work started to sell, he would ask Rushmi to cut back on her hours and, ultimately, give up the job altogether. This was another one of his daffy dreams no doubt, but it felt good to be dreaming again, to experience the pleasure of doing rewarding work.

Bob Wilson, out on bail, called once in a while to talk about their job-related problems. Bob was also having a hard time finding work.

'How's Janet?' Dev asked him.

'Dunno,' Bob said.

'Are you still seeing her?'

'Naaah,' Bob said. 'Can't afford her. Keeping her wined and dined and recreated got to be too expensive. I could spend bucks like that when I was bringing them in, but now—I'm barely able to feed myself and pay the rent.'

'I know,' Dev said. 'Same here. The only bright spot in my life is the watercolors that I'm painting.'

'I've gone golfing several times,' Bob said. 'But even that is more than I can afford.'

'Cheer up,' Dev told him. 'Things are bound to get better.'

He tried to inject a note of enthusiasm into his voice. But he didn't think he sounded very convincing.

'Bye, now,' he said. 'Hope I'll be seeing you soon.'

And he did, but not the way he thought he would. Not many days later, Dev flipped on the TV and saw Bob's face plastered on all the local channels. Another crisis had erupted at Techware. Reporters were transmitting special reports from the company parking lot.

'Shit!' said Dev, sitting down in front of the set. 'I had a feeling this might happen. Even a brain-damaged donkey could have predicted this.'

Bob had, apparently, flipped out again. He had barricaded himself inside the building and was shooting at anything and everything he could see from his position. A dozen or so Techware employees were still in the building, being held as hostages. Dev heard the details repeated over and over again on TV. All the area TV stations had commentators on the scene, reporting on Bob's insane rampage, interspersed, of course, with the usual inane commercial messages.

Bob had gone back to Techware as though he were the Lord of Death. He had taken a duffle bag filled with automatic rifles, shotguns, pistols, hand-grenades, bandoliers of shotgun shells and bullets and even a machete. Cameras with telephoto lenses caught him as he walked past glass windows, dressed in camouflage fatigues. Bent on doing the Rambo thing, he'd even gone to the trouble of dressing up for the part.

The scene had an air of filmic unreality. Could the whole thing be a made-for-TV movie, featuring lackluster talent picked up at random from some street corner?

Television tended to make even serious situations look like staged events with make-believe car crashes and pretend death scenes. Sane people knew that once the scenes had been played out, the actors would get up, dust themselves, go take showers and sit down for dinners with family members.

But this wasn't a low-budget movie. His churning guts, sweaty palms were all the proof he needed. A friend and a colleague stood at the mouth of Hell. He could have already killed people—Dev had no doubt— and he wanted to be killed.

The minions of the Law, now encircling the building, were on hand to make sure that he got his wish.

Some workers had managed to escape, according to the TV commentators, but others were still trapped on the upper floors. A helicopter tried to land on the roof to evacuate them, but Bob fired at it from a balcony. The helicopter veered away sharply, started spinning out of control and went careening to the ground. Fire-engines and paramedics screamed towards the wreckage.

The TV crews were hard on their heels.

Dev wondered how long this would go on.

Professional negotiators had been sent for. Bob had asked for a TV newsman to come in and interview him so that he could tell his side of the story. For a doomed man to be so concerned that his final message to the world be reported right seemed rather odd to Dev.

Meanwhile, the SWAT teams busied themselves, positioning sharp-shooters and gathering and setting up all kinds of equipment to prepare for an all-out assault. Obviously, they wanted to get the 'situation' over with in a hurry. The longer the crisis continued, the more impotent and silly they looked. The matter had to be resolved, wrapped up, handled. The man had to be neutralized before the 5 o'clock news on TV. The forces of Law 'n' Order had to emerge as victors from this fracas.

Dev wanted to turn off the TV, to somehow stop the nightmare as it unfolded with its own slow but irresistible logic. But he couldn't. A sick curiosity, a ghoulish need to see blood spilled, held him in an iron grip.

He wondered if Bob would listen to him if he raced over to Techware, commandeered a bull-horn and begged him to surrender.

Bob, this is Dev. Remember me? I had the cubicle next to yours. Stop this madness, Bob. Surrender. No matter how bad it is, I'm sure there is a way out. Please, Bob, listen to me. I beg you.

Or words to that effect.

Bob would probably respond with a volley of rifle-fire. Fuck off, he'd probably say. I'm sick and tired of being

pushed around. I've had it up to here. I don't give a shit
what happens anymore. I'm already dead, so what the hell.
Take this and this and this, you lousy bastards. You aren't
going to catch me alive.

This is like the Wild West, Dev thought, like the pioneer
days. The time-honored tradition of dying in a hail of bullets.
All we need is background music and this could be one of
those Italian cowboy movies in which the slow motion
choreography of violence and death has a fateful inevitability.

By now the cops were lobbing tear gas canisters into the
building. The SWAT team guys were running around in
hideous pig-snout gas masks preparing to enter the building.
Shots were fired at them from inside the building, but no
one went down. Then, a kind of silence fell over the scene.
Even the fire-trucks and ambulances stood silent, as if waiting
for the next shot to be set up by the 'Director.'

With a supreme effort of will, Dev got up from the couch
and turned off the TV. He'd seen enough. He already knew
what would happen next. He went into the tiny guest
bedroom which served as his studio and turned on the work-
light. He knew what the guys in white coats would find
when they entered the building after the tear gas had
dissipated. They'd find an actor who had been playing a role
in a lousy movie. They wouldn't find Bob, his old friend
and ex-colleague. Bob would be in some place faraway.

Dev took out a fresh sheet of watercolor paper and quickly
drew a single rose on the white surface. Then he picked up a
No. 8 Sable brush and started to add colors to the sketch,
blending them carefully, letting them mix here and there to
form new tints, slowly filling the blank emptiness in front of
him with the image of a flower that would never wither,
never die.

The King of Patio World

Kermool Berbarrian looked intently at his craggy, Mediterranean visage in the bathroom mirror and adjusted his recently-purchased hairpiece. He resembled the guy in that TV show, M.A.S.H., the one who wears women's clothes in the hopes of getting an insanity discharge from the Army. The five o'clock shadow on his swarthy cheeks never went away, no matter how hard he scraped with his razor. And his grandiose Roman beak would have made Julius Caesar snort with pride.

Kermool wanted to impress the female job applicant, who sat waiting in the front office, with his sense of style and elegance. He wore his favorite magenta, polyester leisure suit stitched with contrasting orange thread. His shirt was open at the throat, as always, since he despised neckties. A rather intense yellow with blue polka dots, it had long collars like the ears on a spaniel. And around his neck, he wore several gold chains and medallions that twinkled amidst the cluster of curly, dark hair on his chest.

Satisfied with his appearance, Kermool emerged from the Men's Toilet with a springy step. Rather overly-conscious of being only five feet two inches, he always tried to walk extra straight to make himself look taller.

'Well, Miss—it is Miss, isn't it?—Miss Esmerelda Potts. Esmerelda? That's a rather fancy name? Nice, though, nice...'

The applicant, an exceedingly thin and flat-chested girl, shifted in her chair and crossed her legs.

'My mother found it in a book,' she said with a tentative smile. 'It's French, I think.'

'Well, Miss Potts, from your résumé...you don't really have any experience selling Patio Furniture.'

'But I've worked in several stores. My last job was with a discount fabric outlet.'

'Pardon me,' said Kermool, with a deprecatory shake of his head, 'selling patio furniture is entirely different—a different ball game. See that sign out there. What does it say? "Kermool Berbarrian—King of Patio World." That's me. Selling patio furniture is like selling something people don't really have to have—like diamonds. It takes a special type to sell patio furniture.'

'Well, I used to work at the perfume counter in Macy's...'

Kermool sat up straighter in his chair.

'You did? When? Why did you quit?'

Kermool respected famous retail houses. If Miss Potts had sold perfume for Macy's, then she had something going for herself.

'A while back,' said Miss Potts. 'I quit on moral grounds...'

'What do you mean?'

'I quit because they wouldn't stop selling animal furs. I'm against the slaughter of animals, so some rich woman can walk around dressed in the poor creature's fur.'

Kermool moved back into his chair, rather alarmed by Miss Potts' radical views. In his mind, the rich were a race of superior beings who could never do anything wrong. If the wealthy wanted to wear the fur of animals, no one had any business opposing them. On first impulse, he wanted to give Miss Potts a stern lecture about harboring Commy-pinko ideas. But he kept his peace. She was the only job-applicant who had crossed his threshold in three months. He decided to get back to the topic of patio furniture and set aside controversial issues for another time.

'Miss Potts, this business is my entire life. When I took over this corner lot, there was nothing here, just a run-down gas station that nobody wanted. Look at it now .'

He waved a hand dramatically at the vista outside his glassed-in office. His entire inventory could be seen sizzling under the hot sunlight. Every square foot of the paved area was covered with patio furniture. He had round tables, oval tables, square tables, and rectangular tables. He had beach umbrellas, sun umbrellas and awnings of canvas and nylon, in every color of the rainbow. And chairs, all kinds of chairs—deck chairs, pool chairs, dining chairs, chairs to sit in, to lie on, and lounge on.

Kermool Berbarrian's Patio World occupied a corner at the intersection of El Camino Real and Diablo. All the stores and small businesses in this area of San Jose had a rather shabby, sun-blasted look. Prosperity and elegance had bypassed this enclave and now all the structures seemed to be waiting for the blade of a bulldozer to wipe them off the face of the earth. At one point, gas stations stood on all four corners. But only one company had survived the gas wars of the Seventies. Now a Taco seller had taken up the location on the other side of the street from Kermool and the spot diagonally across, still sat empty, littered with weeds, candy wrappers, crunched soda cans and grease-covered metal parts.

'I made this place what it is,' Kermool said. 'I took out the rusting gas pumps and planted beach umbrellas in their place. And this office, with its glass walls on three sides, is ideal. Customers drive up...I can see them from where I sit. I step out and serve them. Just the other day, a guy offered me $100,000 in cash for this business. I said: No. Why did I say: No? Because this isn't just a business for me. This is my whole world. That's why people call me "The King of Patio World." This is my little kingdom and I am the sole ruler.'

Kermool stopped to catch his breath and admire the effect of his words on Miss Potts. Her mouth had fallen open and she looked a little overwhelmed.

Kermool smiled with satisfaction. He had refined, and rehearsed and revised this speech over the years. He knew what kind of effect it had on people. The look of disbelief on Miss Pott's face would eventually turn into one of silent awe and he waited for this to happen. And when Miss Potts's expression changed—right on schedule—he got up from his chair with a decisive air.

'I'll hire you Miss Potts.' he said, looking out on his domain with narrowed eyes. 'Frankly, you are weak in the area of Patio furniture sales, but you've paid your dues at Macy's. With a little training and experience, you should become a first rate Customer Counselor at Kermool Berbarrian's Patio World.'

Miss Potts mumbled something about 'Customer Counselor.' Kermool heard her and turned around, a smug smile curling his lips.

'I knew you would ask me this question,' he said grandly. 'I call my sales people "Customer Counselors." Why?... because, I think the best way to sell is to give good advice. Most customers have to be guided. They come in here, but they don't really know what they want. The job of a Customer Counselor is to guide them to the product that is right for them. When you do that, the customer invariably buys the product. It's that simple. I don't believe in high-pressure sales tactics and all that song and dance stuff. We have the best products in four counties. The goods sell themselves. All I do is guide the customers to the right product.'

Miss Potts nodded eagerly, but the skeptical set of her mouth did not instill confidence in Kermool. Obviously, she hadn't understood a word he'd said.

Kermool imparted more of his wisdom to Miss Potts for a while and then suggested that they step out. He wanted to show her the inventory. The air outside his glass cage of an office was hot and gritty. As soon as he took his first breath, the odors of creosote and diesel exhaust stung his sinuses and a dagger of pain went straight up between his eyes. In the bright California sun, the plastic looked blindingly white, like the bleached bones of animals found on the Mojave desert. And as the sun climbed the sky, the concrete began to get hotter and hotter. The air above the pavement rose in trembling waves, turning the skeletal jumble of chairs, tables and umbrellas into a liquid mirage.

Oblivious of the heat, Kermool, strutted about his realm like a bantam rooster. He caressed the chairs, aligned the tables and straightened the umbrellas. He rattled off model names and product numbers, partly to show off his knowledge and partly in the hope that Miss Potts would remember everything she was hearing. When they finally stepped back into the cool, air-conditioned dimness of the office, Miss Potts' face looked red as a tomato.

'Boy, it's hot out there.' she said, dabbing at her forehead with a cambric handkerchief that she kept up her sleeve.

'Only in the afternoons,' Kermool countered. 'The evenings aren't bad. That's when we get most of our customers.'

'What would you like me to do now?' Miss Potts asked.

'See those steel drawers,' said Kermool. 'They are full of back-orders. I want you to look through them and call the manufacturers and see when we'll get the deliveries. Then call the customers and tell them when they can expect to pick up their orders.'

Kermool was glad he had someone who would handle the drudgery of follow-up. He hated paperwork of any kind and much preferred chatting with walk-in customers.

* * *

For a month, Kermool observed Miss Potts closely. She arrived punctually at 9:00 every morning, took a half-hour break at noon to eat her sandwich and rarely left before 5:30 p.m. She seemed orderly, neat, and quiet. However, in front of customers she became a bit tongue-tied. 'Perhaps, she just needs more time to become familiar with the inventory,' he mused.

But as time went by, Kermool noticed that Miss Potts lacked the aggressive pushiness that he wanted in a 'Customer Counselor.' And he wondered if he'd made a mistake in hiring her. Miss Potts had large, hazel eyes, lank, mouse-colored hair and a thin-lipped, vulnerable mouth that moved in ways that always made her seem nervous. She wore sandals and long, loose, granny dresses made of hand-printed fabrics from places like Guatemala and Sumatra, and dangly, silver earrings. At times she seemed altogether too ethereal and insubstantial, like a fairy princess out of a children's story book. Kermool wondered if she had the 'killer instinct' that made for a good sales person.

He had hoped that as the vacation months of summer got underway, his business would pick up. Folks had more leisure to sit around their pools and backyards. The time between the Fourth of July and Labor Day was his peak sales period. People needed more patio furniture when the holidays began. But, for some reason, this did not happen. If anything, his business experienced a significant drop.

He decided to have a chat with Miss Potts. Perhaps, she had not been as effective as she could be as a 'Customer Counselor.'

Miss Potts regarded Kermool calmly when he outlined the problem and nodded in agreement.

'You are right,' she said. 'Customers seem to staying away in droves.'

'I don't understand what's going on,' Kermool said. 'I *am* the King of Patio Furniture. No one has a larger collection of styles and models. I just don't understand.'

'Plastic,' said Miss Potts. 'Everything you have here is made of plastic.'

'Why, yes,' Kermool snorted. 'It lasts longer in the sun and rain. People want plastic furniture beside their swimming pools. Wood gets discolored, rots, gets splinters. Plastic is durable.'

'You even wear plastic,' Miss Potts continued.

'What do you mean?' said Kermool defensively.

'Polyester pants and polyester shirts,' said Miss Potts. 'That's plastic.'

'So, what's your point?'

'My point is that people are changing. They are tired of synthetic stuff. They want to get back to a more natural

lifestyle, get close to Nature. People are re-discovering
natural fibers like cotton and silk and wool. But when they
come here, all they see is acres of plastic. They don't
understand how this stuff will fit into their back-yards, or
look beside their swimming pools.'

'So?'

Kermool had no idea what she was driving at.

'So, we've got to change our tactics with the changing
times. Having acres and acres of plastic tables and chairs is
just not enough. We've got to create the proper atmosphere.
Make this place look like a green backyard or a cool, shady
nook where a person can read and relax. Right now, with all
the traffic whizzing past on two sides, and the sun beating
down, this is hardly an inviting ambiance.'

Kermool's eyes got wider. No one had ever talked to him
like that before. Miss Potts seemed to be giving him a lesson
on how to sell patio furniture. And she was using big words,
words that he had never heard before.

'What was that last word you said?' he asked. 'What does
it mean?'

He hated to betray his lack of education, but he wanted
to know.

'Ambiance?' she said.

'Yes.'

'It just means your surroundings, the atmosphere you
have all around.'

'Well, there isn't much I can do about that,' Kermool
said, rather testily. 'This used to be a gas station, you know.
And we are in a prime, central location. Having traffic on
two sides is good for us. More people see us as they drive
by.'

'Fine, but we can change the mood of this place. Make it
prettier, more inviting.'

'How?'

'I have some ideas,' said Miss Potts.

Kermool thought for a while. He did not trust Miss Potts.
She seemed to have been contaminated by wacko ideas that

infected many Californians, especially the tree-hugging, Back-to-Nature types. But he decided to give her enough rope to hang herself.

'All right,' he said. 'What do you have in mind?'

'Greenery,' said Miss Potts. 'We need plants around here. And lots of them.'

'Plants!' yelped Kermool. 'I hate plants. They get in the way. They take up room. They die. I don't want any damn plants around here.'

'Fine,' said Miss Potts. 'But then don't complain if customers stay away.'

'I'll change my product line. I'll get pink and blue and green furniture. I think customers are just bored with white.'

'Go ahead,' said Miss Potts, calmly. 'If there is anything more hideous than white plastic, it's pink plastic. Go ahead, try it. It'll never work.'

'And plants will?'

'You've got to make this place look like a real patio if you want to sell patio furniture. Give people ideas. Show them how they can turn their backyards into magical grottos filled with ferns and palms and flowers.'

Kermool shook his head. Where was she getting all these fool ideas? Grottos? Ambiance? The woman had to be daffy.

'All I ask…look, just let me put some plants around here,' Miss Potts said. 'If things don't turn around, you can throw them out. It's a small investment. But I'm positive we'll start getting some business.'

Kermool looked at her dubiously. Her hazel eyes were bright with a kind inner excitement that he'd never seen in them before. Then just on a whim, just to please her, he said: 'Fine, hand me that check book. Get what you want. But remember, you're the one who's gonna have to water them.'

Miss Potts smiled a mysterious, impish smile.

'There's nothing I like better than watering plants,' she said.

* * *

Miss Potts, started calling nurseries and plant sellers right away. Getting the shrubs, trees and flowers proved to be no problem, but designing a system to water them easily proved a bigger hurdle. Luckily, Kermool decided to come to her aid. A secret tinkerer, he knew how to hook up hoses and pipes and drip systems. In an earlier life, before he became 'King of Patio World,' he'd worked as a low-paid minion at a hardware store. He knew how to connect PVC pipes and set-up sprinklers. Moreover, he figured, he'd better help with the water-system or she'd have pipes bursting all over the place, turning his 'kingdom' into a swamp.

In a little over two weeks, Patio World became transformed into an island of greenery, with flowers of all kinds glittering here and there like gems. Miss Potts chose hardy varieties that needed little or no tending, such as geraniums, nasturtiums and hydrangeas. Along the walls of the office, where she found a strip of soil she planted bougainvillea and honeysuckle. Between the rows of patio furniture, she placed potted ferns, palms and rosemary. She even managed to find room for several orange trees to frame the driveway which gave on to the main road. And along the boundary walls, she planted hedges of myrtle and bay to break the hard-edged, finality of the cinder-blocks. She also had workmen build wooden trellises and pergolas here and there and set up walkways roofed with split-rails that created patterns of dappled light and shade and helped to cool the air.

Even while all this was going on, Kermool sensed a change. When he stepped out of his glass cage of an office, cool, earthy odors greeted him. The dark green foliage of the plants softened the harsh whiteness of the plastic tables and chairs. The furniture seemed to be sitting in its own proper environment.

And then, slowly, gradually, the customers started to come. At first, by ones and twos and then in clusters of four and five. And even though he had Esmerelda to help, he could barely keep up with the flow. Orders began to pile up. Kermool also noticed a change in the way people behaved and reacted. In the past, people used to rush hither and yon, frowning and grimacing in the harsh, intense sunlight. Now, they smiled more and seemed happy and seemed to want to linger and amble around the lot, in a leisurely, relaxed way.

In the new atmosphere, even Miss Potts blossomed. She laughed and giggled more, chatted with customers as though she were meeting long lost friends, and generally seemed happier and more at home. Her long dresses covered with bright prints of birds and butterflies, flowers and leaves, seemed to fit into the jungle green mist that hung over the lot and as she walked about, she seemed to leave behind odors of Alyssum, Honeysuckle and Rosemary.

Kermool began to see Miss Potts in a new light. She had certain talents and strengths that he had not noticed before. She certainly loved plants and flowers and shrubs and trees with an intensity that verged on mania, but she also had a knack for handling people. Customers, both male and female, seemed to like dealing with her. She could win over a person by offering a chair or pointing out a durable awning. Even tired and grumpy customers, became friendly and pleasant in her presence.

By the time summer drew to a close, Kermool found that they had sold more furniture than he had ever sold in the entire previous year. Manufacturers were inviting him to conferences to give speeches on how he had managed to turn things around. From the 'King of Patio World' he was rapidly being transformed into 'Marketing Wizard.'

With money pouring in, Kermool began to treat Miss Potts more and more as a partner instead of an employee. On Friday nights, he started taking her out for meals at a nearby Chinese restaurant. Since he lived alone in a small, bachelor pad, and rarely cooked, he didn't see any point in inviting her to his own place.

He would talk to her about the business and how they were doing and what they could do to speed up orders. But once all the shop-talk had been taken care off he would move the conversation around to personal matters. Did she have a boyfriend? Why hadn't she gotten married? What kind of men did she like?

Miss Potts always gave vague, evasive answers to these questions. She seemed reluctant to dwell on her past. He figured she'd been through some painful scenarios and did not wish to revisit them.

One Friday night, after one of these dinners, rather exalted by Egg Foo Yung and beer, Kermool grabbed Miss Potts' hand in the parking lot and kissed it impulsively. Then, confused and speechless, he raced to his car and made a speedy getaway.

Next day, Miss Potts made no mention of his odd behavior, nor did he bring it up. But he sensed in his heart that she knew something had changed between them, a new factor had come into the balanced equation that had been their relationship. Alone in his room at night, he'd recall how soft her hand had felt, and his heart would thrash about like a fish out of water.

It actually amazed Kermool that he could be attracted to Miss Potts. He had never considered her to be his type. In the past, he would not have looked twice at someone like her. He'd been trained from boyhood on to respond to flashy, buxom, bossomy blondes with garishly lipsticked mouths and muscular thighs, the kind of creatures that Adult magazines featured in their centerfolds. But Miss Potts? She had a frailness and evanescence that almost made her invisible in strong light. Miss Potts only seemed real in a lawn chair, with a wide-brimmed straw hat on her head, surrounded by ferns and potted palms.

And yet, he could not deny the feelings that she had begun to rouse in him. Perhaps Patio World needed a Queen. As the King of Patio World, maybe he needed to think of having heirs, someone who would inherit the business.

While he was struggling with these emotions, something happened that filled him with anxiety.

One morning Miss Potts announced that she had to go to Kansas City. Her mother was very ill and needed her.

'For how long will you be gone?' Kermool asked, his heart sinking to his socks.

'I don't know,' Miss Potts said. 'It could be for a week or so, or much longer. Maybe a couple of months.'

'But I need you here, Esmerelda,' said Kermool.

'I know,' said Esmeralda. 'But I can't just turn my back on my mother.'

'You have your own life to live,' Kermool went on.

'But I feel responsible for her....'

'Perhaps your mother needs to be in a home for the elderly. They have trained nurses, the proper facilities....'

'I guess. I'll have to look into that,' said Miss Potts. 'It might take a while to make the arrangements. But I also have other responsibilities.'

By now Kermool's heart was jumping up and down his throat like a frog, and his ears were filled with loud noises that he could not identify. He grabbed her hand and pulled her close to himself.

'Other responsibilities? What does that mean?' Kermool, asked. A terrible fear filled his chest. Is she going to admit to being married, having a husband somewhere?

Miss Potts looked down at her sandals again and remained silent for a while.

'I have a child, a son,' she finally said. 'He's six. My mother's been looking after him.'

Kermool exhaled in relief.

'What about his father...your husband?'

'I was never married to his father. Our relationship never got to that point. I don't even know where he is now. But we did manage to produce Charlie.'

Kermool looked off towards the shadow-dappled apron of concrete where his furniture twinkled behind scrims of leaves and palm fronds.

'Well,' he said. 'Bring Charlie with you when you come back. I know you'll be able to help him grow. You have the knack.'

'I may have to,' Miss Potts murmured. 'Mom has some type of Cancer. I don't think she is going to be around for very long.'

'Come back as soon as you can,' Kermool said in a choked, husky voice. 'Patio World needs a Queen.'

Kermool saw sudden tears collecting in Miss Potts's eyes. She quickly looked down.

'You can always hire someone else,' Miss Potts said.

'I don't think I'll ever find anyone as capable as you. I need you. I want you back. Promise. You will come back, won't you?' Kermool stopped. He was breathing hard as though he had run a couple of miles.

He had never made a more romantic speech to another living soul.

'I will,' he heard her murmur.

He wanted to say more but his brain seemed unable to formulate sentences and a kind of tremor afflicted his vocal chords. And then he brought an arm around Esmerelda and hugged her. She inclined her head until it rested against his shoulder. The medallions he had awarded himself, tinkled among the chains like wind-chimes with every move he made, providing a muffled fanfare for the royal couple.

The Maid who had Imagination

Rosa tried hard to stay out of the way of the guests at the Pensione Hernandez in Caldelas. She did her work—making beds, dusting rooms, helping out at mealtimes—with such quiet efficiency that, at first, I hardly knew she existed. When I did run into her one day, dusting my room, she did not seem the type who'd attract attention. Rather a plain, almost homely-looking girl with small, close-set black eyes and a thin-lipped mouth, she walked around with her head down. And she always wore shapeless dresses and heavy aprons as if she were determined to hide her figure.

At some very subconscious level, Rosa's simplicity and ordinariness filled me with a sense of relief. I was glad she wasn't a raving beauty or Miss Portugal or something. I neither wanted nor needed distractions like that. I'd come to this tiny village in northern Portugal to simplify my life, not to complicate it. The sick and the ailing had been coming here since Roman times to take the waters and bathe in the medicinal hot springs. But my malaise, as it turned out, happened to be more mental than physical. Instead of drinking the water, I turned to the green vineyards, the pine-scented air and the quiet routines of the spa for relief.

Getting here had not been easy. From Porto, I caught a noisy, jittery little train which took three and half hours to get to Braga. In Braga I had to switch to a bus and endure another three hour haul over twisty mountain roads, stone bridges and swift-running streams. By the time the bus pulled into Caldelas, it was late afternoon and the sun sat low on the horizon. Blue shadows were pooling up in the valleys and a honey-colored light lit up the tops of trees and hills.

The village itself did not look impressive: just a cluster of shops and restaurants around a kind of central square where buses halted to drop off and pick up passengers. Plastic tables, chairs and CINZANO umbrellas of the cafes spilled onto tree-shaded terraces. The locals sat here all day, eating and drinking and watching travellers come and go. On the northern edge of this plaza stood a small grey-stone church steeped in the shade of ancient cork trees.

A friend in Porto had recommended the Pensione Hernandez. So as soon as I got off the bus, I made an effort to find the place. I checked with some idlers hanging around the cafes, but my lack of Portugese and their ignorance of English eliminated all possibilities of communication. Finally, a waiter, with whom I managed to exchange a few words in my mangled French, pointed towards a narrow, unpaved trail. I thanked him profusely, shouldered my satchel and clambered up the slope with a will. Steep and muddy and punctuated with smooth, wet stones, the path made for difficult going as it curled up and around the mountain. Luckily, I had to follow it for only a few minutes, before encountering my destination.

Built out of rough-hewn stones, the Pensione Hernandez seemed neither very large nor very grand, but it did have a marvellous location. The entire structure teetered precariously on a rocky outcropping overlooking a broad valley which fell away sharply and then rose again in a series of undulating folds and terraces to a horizon of distant hills. The slopes were covered with a dense forest of pines, cork-oaks and elms, but here and there one could see orderly vineyards and well-tended vegetable gardens.

Mrs Hernandez, an elderly lady with steel-grey hair, greeted me warmly and assigned me a room with a fine view of the valley. And in a couple of days, I settled into the quiet, comfortable routines of the establishment. My room contained a chair, a table and a small bed, plus a large, old-fashioned armoire. The armoire stood almost six feet high and dominated the room. It had the look of a priceless antique about it and one of its door panels was covered with a huge plate-glass mirror.

Since the price of the room included meals, I hardly ever ate out. Breakfast, served at eight, included coffee, buttered rolls, jam and cold cuts with cheese. A hot lunch came promptly at noon and dinner followed at six sharp. At each meal, my hosts set a tall bottle of cold, crisp white wine before me and I could consume as much as I wanted. Produced locally and known as 'vigne verde' or green wine, this marvellous beverage complemented Mrs Hernandez's cuisine very nicely.

Besides myself, the pensione had only five other 'guests.' A rather over-weight farmer and his wife occupied a room on the ground floor. The farmer had come for a regimen of the waters to repair his digestive system. His ailment must have been serious. He locked himself up in the bathroom at odd hours of the night or day for long stretches of time and I'd hear him groaning and moaning.

Besides this pair, we had one other family at the pensione: an elderly shopkeeper from the southern town of Moura who had brought along his wife and daughter. Rather thin and frail, the man from Moura spoke very little and kept to his room most of the time. I got the feeling that a wasting disease afflicted him and was sapping his strength. But his daughter, a pretty and vivacious girl of about twelve or thirteen, was full of boundless energy. She soon made friends with the neighborhood children and spent her days playing games of hide-and-go-seek with them all over the wooded hills.

I did not have much to do in Caldelas. The village lacked places of public amusement such as movie houses, theatres and museums. To find entertainment, one had to improvise, fall back on one's own resources. After breakfast I'd make a round of the four cafes that surrounded the central plaza and have a cigarette and a coffee in each one of them in turn. After lunch, I'd repair to my room to take a nap, write letters and make notes in my journal. In the evenings, I'd venture forth again for a promenade to exchange smiles with the other tourists who were doing the same thing.

One could call it a dull sort of life, but to me this was like being in paradise. With no distractions and pressures, no deadlines and impending meetings, no urgent projects on my hands that required completion, I could day-dream, doze and generally let my mind wander. For the first time in a very long time, I began to take a certain amount of pleasure in simply being alive, in gazing at the blue sky, the green valleys and listening to the clamor of the birds in the vineyards. I could have gone on existing like this for quite a long time, had not a series of events brought drastic changes to the tenor of my nights and days.

* * *

One lazy afternoon, as I lay in bed hovering between sleep and wakefulness, I noticed that the mirrored door of the armoire stood ajar. The maid must have left it open by mistake, I thought, when she'd come to dust the room. I got up and closed it. But the very next day I noticed that the door stood open once again and again almost at exactly the same angle. I closed it and gave it no more thought. But much to my surprise this became a daily nuisance. Every afternoon the door would be ajar and I would have to close it. But finally all this got to the point that I gave up on the door and began leaving it just the way it was. I did debate with myself whether I should mention the problem to Mrs Hernandez. But the more I thought of the difficulties I would face in explaining the situation to her in my broken French, the less I felt like bothering her. It also worried me that I might create difficulties for the maid. I might even get her fired or something. In the final analysis, it all seemed too petty an issue to make a big fuss over. After all, I could close the damned door with my foot as I lay on the bed. So I said nothing.

But then, not long after I'd adjusted to this irritant, another peculiar thing occurred.

The dining room happened to be the largest chamber at the Pensione Hernandez, and it was in this room that Rosa served us all our meals. It contained one long refectory table and a couple of small round ones. Normally, I ate by myself at the long table, and the other two families were served at the smaller tables. Quite often, I would be the only one in the dining room, which made for lonely but quiet eating. One day as I was preparing to address my lunch, I noticed that one of the bread rolls had a rather odd shape. These small loafs looked like fat cigars or tiny blimps usually, and were served with every meal. This one, however, looked a little like a tube with a rounded knob or protuberance at one end. I couldn't help but think that it looked like a crude representation of a penis. Smiling under my mustache, I pondered the matter for a while. But then, with a kind of grim delight, I broke up the odd-looking roll to sop up my gravy and finished the lunch.

The rolls were baked daily in the Pensione Hernandez. Undoubtedly, someone with a careless hand had created this shape by chance. I gave the matter no more thought and went up to my room.

At dinner that night, I again found a roll that looked distinctly like a penis. I cast my eyes about cautiously to see if anyone else in the dining room had noticed something odd. But the others were busy eating. Nor did it look as though anyone had seen anything out of the ordinary. I examined the roll carefully, turning it this way and that. Once again it had that peculiar cylindrical shape with the knob at one end. But this time the round protuberance at the end also had a tiny slit which made the resemblance to the male organ all the more complete. I had no doubt in my mind that someone had deliberately created this *objet d'art* and set it in my bread basket as a special message or joke. But who could be so audacious, I wondered?

When Rosa came to clear the table, I tried to catch her eye to see if she had some knowledge of what was going on. But her face was calm and free of any expression or emotion and she kept her eyes averted the way she always did.

I decided to try and forget the incident. It had all the characteristics of a childish prank. Perhaps some youngsters were helping out in the kitchen and when they got bored with all the cutting and peeling they resorted to these rural jests. The best course, I decided, was to ignore the whole thing, pretend I hadn't noticed anything. Pranks like these generally lose their sting if the intended victim fails to respond in the expected manner.

Over the next few days the penis-like bread-rolls became bigger and more realistic-looking. In fact, glazed and browned to a turn, some of them could have passed for substantial-looking dildoes. But determined as I was to enjoy the joke instead of accepting the role of a victim, I bit into these items with gusto.

Then one day, just as suddenly as these sexual artifacts had appeared, they vanished, and the bread basket contained nothing more nor less than the ordinary cigar-shaped loafs. When Rosa came to clear the table, I grinned at her rather pointedly, thinking that I had won a small but significant victory. But her face remained expressionless as she went about with her work.

A few days went by without any incident until I realized one morning that I needed to get some underwear laundered. I consulted with Mrs Hernandez in my crude French and by dint of waving a wrinkled shirt and pointing vigorously I managed to make my meaning clear. She, in turn, pointed to Rosa. I should give my clothes to her. She would take care of everything. I did as I was told, thinking that the clothes would be sent to some automated laundromat somewhere. But the very next day, as I walked along the country lane that led to the central plaza, I came across Rosa busily doing the wash near a stone trough fed by one of the hot springs which had made Caldelas famous.

And later on in the afternoon I saw my underwear fluttering merrily in a neighboring vineyard.

I found this rather embarrassing. So next day when Rosa brought back my undershirts and jockey shorts, all neatly ironed and pressed and folded in a tidy bundle, I told her (in plain English) that I'd made up my mind to rinse out my clothes myself and that I had not relished having my underwear put on public display. She understood not a word and retreated from my room all smiles and eloquent hand-gestures as though I had complemented her on something.

I shrugged and started to put away the newly-washed items in the big armoire. About half way through the pile, I noticed a girl's underpants, all pink nylon and a froth of white lace, interleaved between my white cotton briefs. Rather taken aback, I stared at the fragile-looking object for a long time. It had obviously become tangled in my things by mistake. Nor had I any doubt that they were Rosa's. They were too dainty and delicate to belong to an older woman.

As I stared at this article of feminine clothing, trying to comprehend the situation, I began to sense Rosa's presence, her sexual presence in the room. Until now I had successfully relegated her to a marginal existence, as though she were a convenient tool or a machine that performed certain tasks. But now, as I touched those pink panties, her femininity detached itself from her function and assumed a separate identity. Shaking off the shapeless clothing, Rosa emerged naked and free before me, a young woman with normal needs and desires. My ears burned red and I became aware of a pulse throbbing somewhere near my throat.

Not knowing what else to do with the delectable garment, I decided to find Rosa and personally give back her property. I picked up the silken concoction, folded it and held it against my chest with my right hand underneath my jacket. I didn't want to be seen walking around with it, should someone run into me in the hallway.

Rosa happened to be in the room directly across the hall from mine which was unoccupied at the time. The door was ajar. I knocked softly and walked in.

'Rosa,' I murmured.

She turned towards me.

'*Si, senor,*' she said.

Before answering her, I closed the door behind me. Again, I had no desire to be seen waving women's undergarments around in broad daylight.

'*Par erreur,*' I said and drew the pink formulation of lace and silky nylon from beneath my armpit.

Rosa made a little sound, hung her head and reached out. Our fingers touched briefly as the garment changed hands. At that moment I knew as surely as I existed that the presence of Rosa's panties among my underthings had been no accident. She had planted them there as a coded message, a reminder, a sign. It occurred to me that, all along, she had been trying to say something to me. But I had been too dull-minded and stupid, too obtuse and insensitive to catch the meaning of her signals.

Unable to say anymore due to the onset of erratic breathing, I backed out of there and returned to my own room. Then to calm myself and clear my head, I went for a long walk.

I realized that I had a dilemma on my hands. Since I had no knowledge of Portugese and Rosa knew no English, any communication in words was out of the question. The symbolic messages she had been sending were finally reaching me, but I still wasn't sure how to proceed. My status as a 'guest' and as a foreigner placed me at a great distance from her. And her role as a functionary of the establishment put her in constricted circle into which I could not step, at least not in front of others. If I approached her in public, it would be seen as an unpardonable breach of social norms and local etiquette. Any liaison with Rosa would have to be a deep, dark secret, something conducted and consummated in the dead of night. Silence and discretion would have to be major elements of our desperate conjugation.

Several days went by as I brooded over my problem. Not having much else to do, I took my time to examine the situation from every angle. But struggle as I might, I could not think of any way of approaching Rosa without running the risk of offending everyone at the Pensione Hernandez.

Then, quite unexpectedly, something happened which took control of my fate with such sudden directness, that I could no more call my destiny my own than a fallen leaf can, as it is blown about by the wind.

One rather sultry summer night, I lay on my bed trying to stay cool. I had turned off the light and left the door of my room open to let in more air. The pensione was still and silent as a tomb, since everybody had retired for the night. I heard a dog bark on someone's farm. The only other sound was the noise of insects buzzing and the distant lowing of cattle. Then somewhere in the dark valley, a car engine whined as though it were pulling up a steep grade. In this uneasy vacuum of silence, my ears picked up the muffled sound of bare feet slapping against the smooth linoleum in the corridor. Then I heard the door across from my room opening. Exactly at that moment I realized that the door of the large armoire, the one with the tall mirror, which always stood ajar, now afforded me a clear view directly into the room across from my room.

Startled by this realization, I sat bolt upright in bed. I could see nearly all sections of the room across the corridor. A broad band of moonlight coming in through a window illuminated the interior with an eerie bluish-white light. I saw a vague form moving about. It was Rosa. I could see her reflection quite clearly in the deep mirror of the armoire and as I watched her with bated breath, I slowly came to understand a lot of things which had been mysterious and meaningless before. What had seemed random and accidental turned out to be planned and pre-meditated. Rosa had created an elaborate language of signs and symbols, a veritable semiology, to bridge the chasm of estrangement between us.

She stood by the open window for a minute looking out into the night with her back towards me. Then she reached up, unpinned her hair and let it fall down her back in a dark cascade. Her arms gleamed whitely in the moonlight. Then quite casually, she turned around, undid the stays of her dress and let it fall in a puddle of fabric at her feet. Her body glowed in the ambient darkness like marble. She was utterly naked and when she turned again and stood in profile to me as she combed her hair, I could see her breasts tremble and quiver with every movement of her arm.

I felt myself being overwhelmed by an acute anxiety. My mouth felt dry as a desert and my heart thudded wildly in my chest. I wondered if this were an invitation. I wondered what would happen if I approached her. The consequences of a mistake, a miscalculation, a misunderstanding would be catastrophic. Could I have misread all the cues, misinterpreted all the signs? Were my own dire needs leading me into folly? In the final analysis, there was only one way to find out the truth, to discover the ultimate reality. I would have to get up and follow Rosa, go wherever she led me. I could see the gentle curves of her youthful body clearly as she stood there combing her hair. A tendril of cool air reached out from her room towards me, bringing the smell of a light, flowery perfume, something French and sensuous. Unable to wait anymore, I decided to take a chance. I got up like a somnambulist and walked straight into the deep mirror in front of me, the shadow-world where Rosa existed as an image of forbidden desire.

Slouching Towards San Hozay

'General Cheshire!' I shouted into the microphone, 'send us reinforcements. Please. We're in deep trouble.' My voice, pitched high, must have sounded hysterically feminine. But I was past the point of caring. 'They are coming at us from every side,' I shrieked. 'We can't hold out much longer.'

I was not exaggerating, in sooth. The Guerillas had turned our flank and were now threatening our lines of supply. I simply had to get through to the General. But this was proving more and more difficult. I waited by the wireless set. Thirty seconds elapsed. Then a whole minute went by. I could hear nothing but the whine and static of banshee frequencies. The Guerillas were probably jamming our transmission. This was my third attempt that day to get in touch with our Great Leader. The wireless was the only link between us and his headquarters in the Catalina foothills north of Tucson. Our runners had all been cut down by the Guerillas. They were using REAL ESTATE AGENTS and USERERS to do their dirty work. It had become clear to us that if the Great Cheshire didn't get his ass in gear right away our goose was as good as char-broiled.

My aunts and cousins have always believed that in the arena of life, my fate would be that of the victim. Time and events, I'm afraid have proved them right. However, in San Hozay you don't have to be a weakling to develop a healthy fear of Guerillas. The entire city reeks of their presence. They have a peculiar odor: a blend of Eau de Soixante-Neuf, navel lint and polyester. There's no escaping it. Winds from the Bay, heading south towards the NO-MAN'S-LAND of Gilroy and Morgan Hill waft it over our bunkers. The smell makes our wives restive. They go into frenzies. The Guerillas are cunning. They know our weaknesses.

Around dusk, when the sun sinks behind the Santa Cruz mountains, and oblique shafts of amber light set afire the autumnal foliage of apricot groves, the Guerillas take to the expressways and thru-ways in their souped-up vans, pick-up trucks and Chevies. They show no respect for the sanctity of the Violet Hour, which we have set aside for the consumption of tranquil martinis. They cruise up and down the streets in vehicles with very fat tires in the back, tires with white lettering on them. They peel rubber at traffic lights and pull wheelies right in our backyards on dirt-bikes without any mufflers. These tactics tend to increase the restiveness of our wives.

I wanted to tell General Cheshire that we were fast approaching the end of our endurance. I wanted to tell him that we had even tried to communicate with the Guerillas, (the IRS is my witness) to open a dialogue with their Chiefs. But these efforts proved fruitless. The Guerillas had never heard of *Détente*. They did not know French.

The principal problem which plagued our negotiators was that the Guerillas had no taste. We sent them gifts of fine woolens from Saks and I.Magnin, but they returned the boxes unopened with terse notes which said: 'We prefer double-knit polyester ready-mades from Hong Kong.' Undismayed we instructed our representatives to discover other areas where we might seek common interests. Music, our Agents informed us, could be used to promote Harmony. After all, it was a universal language.

The Guerillas apparently possessed a primitive, basic form. But one could hardly refer to it as music. We would often hear their tom-toms going far into the night, insistent, pulsating. The sound made our wives very restive and they would begin to whinny and nicker and paw the ground. This proved most embarrassing. However, the fact remained that Guerilla music lacked Intellectual frisson. We issued orders for amplifying systems to be set up all along our border adjacent to Guerilla territory. We were determined to enrich their lives. From dawn to dusk we broadcast the creations of our Great Masters. Imagine our surprise when the Guerilla Chieftains sent us a delegation bearing threats of massive retaliation. They promised to bomb our suburban tract homes with 77.7 mm Sausages and megatons odd Derision if we refused to stop our musical attack.

We were depressed to see that the Guerilla delegations carried very ugly luggage. So we procured for them fine suitcases made of Italian Gigolo hides cured in Muscatel, bags lined with the fur of endangered species, trunks ribbed with whalebone. But when the Guerilla delegates returned to their headquarters—located in the parking lot of Bob's Burger Heaven—with their new luggage, they were charged with Malfeasance and Bad Faith and fired on the spot.

This was the last straw, to coin a phrase. The Guerillas had insulted us. They had rejected our Lifestyle. It was widely felt among our Elders that this kind of behavior could not, indeed, should not, go unpunished. Our Committee on Insatiate Aggression (CIA) voted to abandon *Détente* and take up Confrontation. Our Generals were elated. A war at last! Something to fill the long, empty days.

Our Committee on Insatiate Aggression issued a general call to arms. The Guerillas would have to be pacified for their tasteless ways. We could not allow their Bad Taste to spread and flourish unchecked, to infect our lives, nay, to corrupt the lives of our children! We summoned our womenfolk and ordered them to get ammunition. They repaired forthwith to the Magazines. Eagerly they pored over the latest issues of *Vogue, Cosmopolitan, Harper's Bazaar* and *House Beautiful.* Soon their acquisitive instincts had been aroused to an incredible pitch by sophisticated advertising techniques.

We felt confident that when we unleashed our Purchasing Power the Guerillas wouldn't have a prayer.

As it turned out, our optimism was misplaced. We had not taken into consideration their ability to survive. We also discovered that we were no longer the strong nation we had thought we were. Most of our menfolk between the ages of

35 and 45 had been weakened by the sensation of being de Trop. This disease of Terminal De Tropness was an epidemic against which we could find no antidote. These factors damaged our Fall Offensive Strategy.

'Great Leader!' I screamed into the microphone. 'We cannot handle the mortgage payments, and the miasma of Urban Cowboyism which lies thick upon the land, is suffocating us. The air-waves are crammed to capacity with the peculiar, metronomic chants of these Guerillas. And they keep dumping this garbage on us by the Kilohertz. It's not possible for us to hold out much longer.'

Once again: no response from Tucson. Could it be that our Great Leader had been kidnapped by the valkyries who have their lairs in the Red Light district of Nogales?

'Sdeath! I muttered to myself. What will become of us now? How can our people struggle against the Guerilla Counter-Culture without proper guidance? Our people needed, nay deserved, a charismatic leader. General Cheshire (even the foe admits) was indeed such a one. His smile was famous all over the Southwest. Bemused. Tolerant. With a hint of mockery beneath the heavy mustache.

The enemy came at us wave upon wave with unrelenting fury. Our menfolk were succumbing all along the battlefront, anaemic and weak from multiple orgasms. And our womenfolk were more restive than ever. In fact, (and I admit this to our eternal shame) some of our women were functioning as a Fifth Column. (I hope this information never falls into enemy hands.) We caught a few fraternizing with the Guerillas. They were exchanging recipes and telephone numbers of baby-sitters!

Then the Panty Raids began. They almost broke the back of our Defense Strategy. It became clear to the Committee on Insatiate Aggression that we would have to use the Nuclear Family as a weapon. The Guerillas had pushed us to the limits of our tolerance. We had tried everything else.

We had bombed their discobunkers with Gucci loafers and Pucci scarves. We had laid down a barrage of Inanities and Persiflage. We had tried to smother them with Harris Tweed and Crepe de Chine. And for a while it looked as though our tactics were working. The canvasses of Kandinsky and Miro which we exhibited in their arrondissements had a devastating effect. Hundreds of Guerillas were seen running away in terror. Encouraged by this, we added Dali and Picasso to our arsenal. We even included Magritte and de Chirico, despite the fact that their work causes nerve damage and has been banned by the Geneva Convention on Civilized Warfare. For a while it looked as though we would be able to destroy the Guerillas once and for all. But this was not to be. Alas!

We were betrayed by traitors within our ranks!

These traitors wanted our Universities to hand out Degrees and Diplomas to the multitudinous spawn of the Guerillas. They wanted us to hand out credentials in such areas as Advanced Roller Skating and the Fundamentals of Spirit Healing. But our wise Soothsayers pointed out that there was no precedence for this. However, they were soon silenced by cadres of Militant Suburbanites.

The situation deteriorated very rapidly. We realized that San Hozay was not at all like San Francis. San Hozay was more like an idiot clone-brother of L.A. In San Hozay one could always detect a whiff of violence in the air, a taint of insanity, a tincture of alcoholism and a mile wide streak of ass-holery. The Guerillas had infiltrated all the Public Sector jobs in town and most of the Federal Agencies. San Hozay was not mellow. No one in San Hozay knew the meaning of the word 'mellow.'

I wish I had been able to contact General Cheshire. I wanted to tell him that the Guerillas had turned fruit orchards into condominiums, parking-lots and taco stands. We had tried to stop them by throwing the works of Blake, Whitman and Thoreau at their bulldozers. But they proved immune to our weapon systems. Then our Soothsayers suggested that we try more scientific methods. So we mined their discobunkers with electronic games and bombarded

them with computerized Teddy bears. Our forces were
heartened.

We celebrated our gains by drafting all twelve-year old
males who were at least physically fit. General Cheshire had
taught us that the best possible thing we could do was to
sacrifice our lives for mortgage payments. Our brave children
believed this implicitly. With happy hearts they marched
forward to defend our border. Unfortunately, they could
not find the border. By now the monsoons had set in and
where our border used to be, only some anonymous rocks
and stones remained. This unexpected development
undermined the morale of our sub-teen fighters. Here we
had batallions of rosy-cheeked, twelve-year olds ready and
willing to lay down their lives in defense of our border and
now the border could not be found. We ordered the
Committee on Insatiate Aggression to conduct an inquiry.
We wanted them to discover the whereabouts of our border.
The Committee pondered the matter and then broke for
lunch.

I cannot speak much longer. The battle is going badly
for us.

Here in the trenches Time passes with alarming rapidity.
Fellows who were sprightly young bucks one day, discover
that they've turned into toothless, wrinkled old Has-beens
the very next. Fresh, tender young girls, turn into shagged-
out crones overnight. No one knows why this is happening.
The Soothsayers blame the vanishing ozone layer. Our
morale is sinking.

Sources close to the Guerilla Chieftains indicate that they
are still not willing to sit down at the Negotiating Table.
They say they do not like the shape of this table. It is
rectangular. They want one with the shape of a banana.

Western observers have observed that the Guerillas have
dry skin. Their pores are starved for emollients. We have
made it known to them that we are willing to supply them
with oil if they would only agree to a cease-fire. So far they
have not responded.

We have noticed a drastic increase in the defection rate of our women. They are clamoring for divorces. This does not surprise us. Life in the trenches is harsh and punishing. Life in the trenches is a seven-to-seven grind with long commutes and hours in traffic-jams. Life in the trenches is cold salami lunches bolted hurriedly during extended bouts with paperwork. Life in the trenches is ulcers, hemorrhoids, lower-back pain, kidney trouble, prostate failure, lung cancer and bad breath. Life in the trenches is going bald before you hit thirty. Life in the trenches is no fun at all. We can hardly blame our wives for wanting to defect. Scores go over to the Other Side every day. They are seeking Political Asylum in the laundromats. We...

President Sahib's Blue Period

*We showed Pharoah Our signs, but he denied
them and gave no heed.* (The Koran 20:36)

President General Sahib, Commander-in-Chief of the Army,
the Navy, the Air Force and the dreaded Civil Sanitation
Police (CSP), Great Leader of this (almost) fictional nation
of Pakypoor, woke up from a deep sleep with a leonine roar
and called for his loyal ADCs. The sound of his voice echoed
through the musty halls of the Government House, set the
compound's archaic mongrels to howling and shook loose
the luminous pigeons that roosted on the dome of the Royal
Mosque, sending them flying in nervous, dipping spirals
around the amethyst skies above the sleeping city of
Islamagood.

'Ho Fazaldeen! Ho Faltoo!' President Sahib shouted.
'Wake up, sons of donkeys! Up, up, you flea-bitten sister-
suckers. I have had a fearful dream and it has dried the
blood in my veins and melted the marrow in my bones.
Rise, you lazy sons of mango-stealing washer-women, or I'll
whip your brown arses till they glow redder than the bottoms
of baboons.'

Fazaldeen and Faltoo, more likely as not, deep in their
own dreams of erotic Hollywood starlets, struggled into
wakefulness and hastened to locate their sandals.

'Faltoo, you pig's pizzle, did you hear me? Get me General
Yahoo Khan on the phone. I am declaring Martial Law. And
I want Yahoo Khan to put the Armed Forces on full alert.
Then get me my hookah and my prayer mat. I must beg
mercy from Allah (the Shelter and Support of Muslims
everywhere) for in my dream I saw such sights as bode ill
for me and the nation of Pakypoor. And you, Fazaldeen,

take my speedy black cadillac and fetch Aboo bin Froydh, the Mullah of Mullahs. Go. Hurry. I fear the hand of Allah's wrath is upon me and my fate may be that of Nimrood.'

In the solemn silence of the purple hours before dawn, all this noise and commotion became greatly magnified and eventually reached the Great Begum Sahiba, President Sahib's first and least favourite wife, as she slept in the *zenanah* or women's quarters surrounded by flocks of brood hens, milch cows, goats, talking parrots, teething infants, grinning cousins, junior wives and assorted aunts, uncles, nieces, nephews and ayahs.

Waking up with a start and fearing the worst, the old Begum grabbed a six-foot bamboo staff (which she always kept at her bedside) and hurried towards the presidential suite as fast as her bunioned feet could carry her.

Nearly ninety, purblind, toothless and almost as wide as she was tall, the old Begum still managed to move around with considerable agility. And she still had a lot of influence over her powerful but erratic husband, a phenomenon for which no one in the Cabinet could find a rational explanation. Rumors circulated in the bazaars and back-alleys of Islamagood that even the Chief Minister, the Right Honorable Nezzar ed Nabook, often begged her to intercede on his behalf when he needed President Sahib's signature on important bills and decrees.

'*La hawl!*' sputtered the Begum Sahiba, pronouncing a spell against the Wicked One. 'What on earth has come over you, Salman's father?'

(Salman, her first-born child of midnight, had been declared a *persona non grata* in Pakypoor. It seems he had earned President Sahib's undying hatred by becoming a very-very modern artist, and painting portraits of his father which made him look like a snake-eyed monster.)

'Has your brain turned into halva?' continued the Begum Sahiba. 'Or have you been drinking that amber liquid sent to you by the American ambassador—that Wilson Barfood—

to befuddle your wits? Tell me, why are you rubbing your forhead into the ground like this?'

'Shut your gums, you rancid witch,' growled President Sahib, displaying a certain highly non-Muslim lack of chivalry. 'Can't you see I am praying?'

'Always rude and crude. Allah, Allah, will this man ever change?' the Begum Sahiba muttered, rolling her eyes upwards. Then she added, 'Don't you know, Salman's father, you have no need to perform this ritual. Remember—you hired all the mullahs in the land to pray for you five times a day. Now let us suppose that there are two million mullahs in Pakypoor, then with a little simple arithmetic—let's see, two times five is ten, that's ten million prayers being said for you every single day!'

Having said this, the Begum placed her enormous bulk upon President Sahib's bed (which creaked loudly in protest) and placidly proceeded to prepare a betel leaf for herself. All the ingredients she needed were in a prettily chased silver container or *paan-daan* which she always carried under her arm. And now she went about the whole procedure with a methodical and exasperating deliberateness. Opening the betel container she removed a single betel leaf from a little stack wrapped in a wet rag which kept them fresh. Then with tiny silver spatulas, she smeared the leaf with slaked lime and the reddish-brown extract of the cashew nut. Next, she sprinkled some slivered betel nut and anis seeds on top of the leaf, added a couple of cloves and cardamom pods, folded the leaf over carefully into a neat packet and popped the whole mess into her mouth.

'Begum, will you stop this cud-chewing, for Allah's sake?' said President-Sahib, striking his forehead with the heel of his right hand in a gesture, both womanish and despairing, which ill-became a man of his stature. 'You know nothing about the perils of State-craft and the constant dangers I must face.'

'Courage, Salman's father!' responded the Begum. 'No one born from woman's womb can harm you. By force of

Arms you gained the highest seat in Pakypoor. You hanged the only man who could have challenged your right to rule. You have all the mullahs and the CSP gang solidly behind you. And even Barfood is eating curried chicken out of the palm of your hand. So why worry your lion-heart about trifles?'

'But, Begum...'

'Pish! You have ruled Pakypoor for many, many years and you will rule it for many more. It is written. This is your kismet. Look—four American presidents have come and gone, three Russian premiers are buried safely in stone mausoleums, two British prime ministers are selling dirty picture cards on the streets of London, and even in Arabia they killed a king and got a new one, but you...you are still head of our poor-but-proud Muslim country.'

'You don't understand, Salman's mother,' said President Sahib, wearily shaking his head. 'This dream that I had has filled my liver with fear and foreboding.'

'A dream? A dream you say?' the Begum snorted sarcastically. 'Why you weak-hearted sparrow, for a moment I was really worried. For one moment I thought that the CSP-wallahs had turned against you.'

The Great Begum feared nothing and no one in the land except the CSP element. Through a skillful combination of bureaucratic chicane and heroic idleness, the CSP had managed to extract wide-ranging powers from President Sahib. And these powers, they never hesitated to abuse.

President Sahib had made the CSP responsible for keeping Pakypoor neat and clean, giving it the charter to remove the dung left behind by the thin ponies that were used to pull public conveyances known as 'tongas.' He also put the CSP in charge of enforcing the regulations against spitting and pissing in public. Such a task might seem thankless and, one would imagine, demeaning. But the CSP performed its duty with much zeal and éclat, going so far as to stage colorful mutilations in front of large and appreciative audiences. If they caught anyone spitting in the street, they cut off the chap's tongue. If they caught a man pissing alongside a public thoroughfare, they cut his... well, you get the point.

The Begum, no longer anxious about the CSP, chided her husband mercilessly.

'Only idiots and suckling infants are frightened by dreams,' she said, aiming a stream of blood-red spittle into a silver spittoon. 'You have nothing to fear as long as the mullahs are praying for you.'

'You don't understand, you blubberous hag,' said President Sahib with mounting irritability. 'Don't you know that dreams often presage coming events? Remember the dreams of the pharoah? Had not Yusef discovered their prophetic meanings, the land of Egypt would have turned into a blasted waste-land.'

'Come, come Salman's father, don't let your head swell up like a goat-skin full of swamp-water,' quoth the Begum. 'A pharoah you are not. And even if you were, we have no Yusef in all of Pakypoor to decipher your foolish dreams.'

'I may not be a pharoah,' said the President huffily, 'but I do think like one. And even though there is no Yusef in the land to interpret my dreams, we do have Aboo bin Froydh, the Mullah of Mullahs. He is a wise and saintly man. He knows how to cast out jinns and read palms. He also knows which verses from the Holy Koran to recite in support of my brilliant and incomprehensible policies. He will be able to tell me the meaning of my dreams.'

'Then send for him, O Leader of the Faithful, but please do stop pointing your posterior towards the sky in this most unseemly manner.'

Even as the husband and wife were concluding their amicable dialogue, the subdued burbling of an automobile engine signalled the return of the presidential cadillac. President Sahib sprang from his prayer mat and raced out to the portico.

'Fazaldeen,' he cried out in great excitement, 'have you brought the Mullah of Mullahs?'

But before Fazaldeen could respond, the back door of the limousine flew open and six midgets tumbled out. They pushed and shoved each other as they emerged, chittering in squeaky, high-pitched voices. All of them looked exactly alike and sported matching dainty white turbans and stylish buff-colored caftans made of fine woolen camlet.

President Sahib staggered back with an oath on his lips.

'By the henna-red beard of my pious grandfather! What jinns and afreets are these, in the name of Sultan Soleyman?' he cried out. 'Answer me, Fazaldeen. I sent you to fetch Aboo bin Froydh and you bring back this litter of midgets. Have you lost your senses, you donkey's hose-pipe?'

'Mercy, President Sahib,' Fazaldeen moaned. 'I did the best I could. Aboo bin Froydh died last year and now in his place these six are considered the Mullah of Mullahs.'

'Do not torment me, Fazaldeen, or I'll flay you alive,' shouted President Sahib.

'As Allah is my witness, I am telling you the truth, Sahib,' said Fazaldeen. 'After Aboo bin Froydh ascended to Paradise, no one could fill his noble caftan. The Great Convocation of Pakypoor mullahs looked far and wide, even as far as Isfahan and Qom. Finally, they selected these six. All together they add up to one Mullah of Mullahs.'

Shocked and disheartened, President Sahib put a hand to his brow and would have fallen to the ground had not Faltoo supported him.

The tiny mullahs, on the other hand, were overjoyed at being inside the Government House. They laughed and clapped their wee hands in utter delight and paid no heed whatsoever to President Sahib. Soon they were chasing each other all over the palace, running wildly through the many labyrinthine passageways and galleries of the enormous structure until they were all good and lost.

Inevitably, a few ended up in the *zenanah* and quickly joined the gangs of mongrels and sub-literate cousins who were busy in games of hide-and-seek under the clotted shade of bearded banyan trees. Some of the wet-nurses mistook the mullahs for over-grown babies and began to suckle them. One or two mullahs objected strenuously and struggled to escape, interlarding their protests with the most hideous oaths which your correspondent cannot set down for fear of offending the Fairer Sex. Others decided to make the best of a parlous situation and accepted the feeding with good grace, thinking (one would imagine) that a free lunch was a free lunch.

Meanwhile, President Sahib paced up and down on the verandah, seething and simmering in a black rage. His skull throbbed painfully and a bulging vein twitched just above his left eye.

'Ho Faltoo, ho Fazaldeen, you degenerate sons of owls!' he shouted, 'get these meddlesome mullahs out of here and tell General Yahoo Khan to come here immediately. I am in the midst of a National Crisis and he is nowhere to be seen.'

It was High Noon by now. The sun stood at its zenith and brown mynah birds with bright yellow beaks were busily mating and quarrelling in the tall tali trees.

'Don't tell that...that Yahoo anything, Salman's father,' said the Begum Sahiba. 'He thinks that you are a private dancing eunuch of the Americans...that you'll shake your hips whenever they throw dollar bills at you.'

'Stop-stop. Don't harass me, woman,' said President Sahib. 'Go and assemble all my wives and children and grandchildren, all my aunts and uncles, nephews and nieces and tell them to mend their ways.'

Deep in his heart, President Sahib had a terrible fear that some day the people of Pakypoor would rise up in revolt against him and his multitudinous and parasitic clan and put them all to the sword.

While he spoke, Fazaldeen and Faltoo lurched about the grounds trying to corral the errant mullahs and stow them back into the presidential cadillac. It took a while to do this because the mullahs proved elusive as bedbugs and just as hard to catch. For a few minutes this sacerdotal hullaballoo threatened to escalate into a full-blown Political Crisis, but suddenly a tremendous wind surged up out of nowhere and came roaring down upon the Government House with the sound of a hundred hurricanes. All the residents of the compound dropped whatever they were doing and came rushing out. But not a cloud could be seen anywhere and the sun shone brightly out of an aquamarine sky. And yet everyone felt this terrible wind tearing at the trees and heard the monstrous roaring.

'Allah! Allah!' the Begum Sahiba cried out in panic. 'What evil storm is this that brings no clouds nor any fertilizing rain?'

The furious wind bent the neem trees over, whipped at the tall cypresses and flailed the talis and peepals. Within seconds all the flower-beds lay ravaged. The zinnias, petunias and pansies were torn up by the roots and scatttered about as if struck by the mephitic breath of some wicked giant.

'Ya Allah, what is this *toophan*?' the Begum Sahiba moaned. 'Is this the Day of Doom? Is Allah going to wipe out the whole of creation, the way he did once before when only the Prophet Noah and the creatures on his ark survived?'

As they all cowered in fear and muttered special prayers, the roaring got louder and louder and the wind more fierce. Even the ancient banyan trees, which had survived a thousand monsoons, swayed and trembled like tender saplings. The old family retainers clutched their turbans and fell flat on their faces and the women and children clung to each other and whimpered behind the potted palms on the verandah.

But then, just when it looked as though the world would indeed blow away, a huge helicopter appeared in the sky and began to descend upon the front lawn of the Government House.

'Fantastic,' said President Sahib, 'All is well. We have nothing to fear. It is the American ambassador himself, coming to see me.'

The ungainly machine which resembled nothing more than a giant mosquito, floated delicately to the ground, its undercarriage flexing and unflexing. As the pilot turned off the engines, the noise and wind died down, bringing into greater prominence the squeals of amazement and alarm emanating from the assembled throng. Then, even as everyone watched awestruck, the door of the helicopter opened, a silver ladder came out and a tall pink-faced man with a white goatee stepped down.

'A-ha,' President Sahib cried out, 'Ambassador Barfood! This is indeed a wonderful surprise. What brings you to my humble compound which you have never graced with your presence before?'

Ambassador Wilson Burford's arrival proved very unsettling for many residents of the Government House. The brood hens clucked loud and long, as did the presidential wives, complaining about ruffled feathers and frayed nerves. Even the somnolent mongrels went into frenzies of hysterical howling which lasted well into the night. And several months later, *The Pakypoor Times*, the nation's leading newspaper (quick as ever to comment on events of national importance) reported that a few wet-nurses had indeed gone quite dry, as had some of the more sensitive water-buffaloes.

Ambassador Burford, all elegance and charm, doffed his black top-hat and extended a glad hand.

'How do you do, President Sahib?' he said, exposing his superlative dental armature in a wide smile.

'I'm fine, I think.' President Sahib responded.

'Good. Good. Lately we have been a little concerned. We sensed a rise in the level of your anxiety. All our sensors and monitors, our computerized measuring devices and detection satellites have been picking up signals which led us to believe that you were getting worried. I have come to give whatever counsel and comfort it is in my power to provide.'

'That is very kind of you, Barfood Sahib. Come, let us go into my office. We can hold our discussions there in comfort and privacy.'

As he turned, he noticed that a crowd still milled around the helicopter, all wide-eyed and gaga.

'Go, go away,' he shouted angrily. '*Jao, jao,* everything is all right.'

But it was only when the Great Begum Sahiba swung her bamboo cudgel menacingly, that the uncles and aunts and their drooling seven-month runts, all fell back and made way for the President Sahib and his supernal guest.

'Ho Faltoo,' President Sahib shouted, 'go and fetch some hot-hot tea for the Ambassador Sahib and tell the Begum Sahiba to relenquish a few of those delicious luddoos and sweet gulab jamuns which I brought from the bazaar just yesterday. Go. Hurry. *Jaldi, jaldi,* quick-quick. Ambassador Sahib doesn't have all day to sit on his thumb waiting for you.'

'That's all right, President Sahib, please don't bother,' said Ambassador Burford.

'No bother-shother at all,' said the President. 'This is just like a family visit. You are father and mother for us, Sahib. And your coming to visit me...why Sir, it is a great honor for me and my unworthy clan.'

Saying this, the President led the way to a small and intimate meeting room where the two sat down face to face on comfortable upholstered chairs.

'Now tell me, President Sahib, what is causing you so much concern that you've set our surveillance satellites buzzing and our computers whirling like dervishes?'

'It's nothing really, Sir. You need not worry about these matters. I can take care of my own affairs.'

'You forget, President Sahib, your affairs are our affairs. After all, we are one big happy family, are we not? And our Grandfather who lives in the big white house across the blue waters of the ocean has asked me to determine what we can do to lessen your anxiety.'

President Sahib squirmed in his chair, looked at his watch, stared up at the ceiling, bit his lower lip and then realizing there was no way out, he finally spoke in a low voice.

'I've had a terrible dream,' he said.

'A dream? Ah, that's good. This verifies what our computers and satellites have been telling us. Now why don't you stretch out on yonder couch and tell me all about this dream.'

'Well, Sir, in this terrible dream I saw that I was in my Cadillac and suddenly it left the ground and began to fly up, up, like an aeroplane, higher and higher above the earth. I felt very happy. But then I looked down and saw that the green and fertile acres of Pakypoor had turned into a howling wildnerness, a barren desert filled with sand and rocks and stones. The mighty Himalayan mountains were bare of trees and grass as are the valleys of the moon and the five great rivers of the Punjab were completely dry. I could not believe my eyes. Then all of a sudden we started to tumble down. I said, "Fazaldeen, what is the matter, why are we falling?" and he turned to me and said, "We have a flat tire, Sahib."'

'But that doesn't make sense,' said Ambassador Burford. 'Only last month we supplied you with four brand new tires as a part of our new aid package.'

'I know it doesn't make sense, Barfood Sahib. This is what worries me. But listen, this was just the beginning. I saw even stranger things.'

'Please continue.'

'The very next instant I found myself in a vast ocean of blood. I swam and swam until my arms were stiff. The slimy red liquid was all over me and I thought I was surely going to drown. But then I saw a golden throne floating on this sea of blood and I began to swim towards it. I reached it after hours of struggle and pulled myself up with the greatest difficulty. I had barely made myself secure upon this throne when I sensed that it was starting to disappear. I suddenly realized that it wasn't made of gold at all but *luddoos*, exactly like these sweetmeats in front of you on this plate, and all kinds of fish, both big and small were nibbling away at it. It became clear to me that very soon it would vanish entirely and I would be back in the sticky red substance.'

Ambassador Burford had been on the point of popping a *luddoo* in his mouth but he changed his mind for some reason and put the delicacy back on his plate. 'This is truly awful. Then what happened, President Sahib?'

'Well, Sahib, I called upon Allah for help and suddenly I realized that I was back in my compound surrounded by my sacred Nili bar water-buffaloes—all five hundred of them. I was happy for a while but then I realized that the animals were starting to shrink. They kept getting smaller and smaller right before my eyes, just like balloons from which air is leaking. I ran up and tried to pinch their nostrils shut, but this did not work. They got smaller and smaller and suddenly changed into crows. I screamed and yelled but there was nothing I could do.'

'How horrible,' said Ambassador Burford.

'Then, Sahib, these crows flew up into the sky and transformed themselves into F-16 fighter airplanes and started to bomb and strafe my compound.'

'How odd.'

'But this isn't all, Ambassador Sahib.'

'You mean there is more?'

'It was all very horrible, Sahib. I cannot tell you how horrible. I started to run in panic, trying to get away from the F-16 fighter planes when a golden eagle landed on my head and began to tear out my brain. I tried to shake it off, but I couldn't. Blood dripped into my eyes and I ran around crazily screaming in pain until I fell down in the dust. When I woke up, I was still screaming.'

Ambassador Burford remained silent for a long time. His blue eyes glittered brightly as he narrowed them in intense concentration and stroked his beard thoughtfully.

'Well, Ambassador Sahib, what do you think of all this? I do not understand these dreams-shreams. But what I saw is causing me much concern.'

Ambassador Burford nodded his head and allowed a little smile to play across his lips.

'And you should be. Dreams are often the precursors of things to come and they should never be ignored or taken lightly. People who think that images seen in sleep are merely fumes and phantasms produced by an over-active digestive system often pay a heavy penalty.'

'What is your advice, Sir? What must I do?'

'It is clear to me, President Sahib, that you are in grave danger. You need more military aid for your protection and for the security of Pakypoor. It is apparent that some Evil Force is contemplating an attack upon you.'

'But Sahib, I already have five hundred F-16 fighter planes, five thousand tanks and many big guns and bombs.'

'That will not be enough,' said Burford Sahib. 'You need five hundred more F-16s and another five thousand tanks. Believe me, one can never have enough tanks and F-16s when it comes to defending one's Life and Liberty from the threat of evil forces.'

'But Sahib, ours is a poor country, we have no petroleum, no gold or uranium mines. How will I ever pay you for all these weapons?'

Ambassador Burford smiled. 'Come now President Sahib, did I say anything about payments? Now don't you worry about that. We are your friends, remember? I would never think of asking you for payment. We've never asked you to pay for weapons in the past. Why would we start asking you now?'

'You are indeed generous, Barfood Sahib. But isn't there anything that I can do for you? Anything? Just tell me what it is. If it is in my power, I will surely do it.'

The Ambassador thought for a while and then he shook his head.

'No, no, President Sahib,' he said. 'You have already done enough for us. The soda-water bottling plants you allowed us to build in Pakypoor....'

'That is nothing, Barfood Sahib. The thanks are due to you. Keep in mind that this is a very hot country and everyone gets very thirsty. I am sure my people are overjoyed and grateful that they can now buy and drink clean, pure soda-water whenever and wherever they desire.'

'Well, I must get back to the embassy, Sahib and order the airlift of all the armaments you need. Remember, we are on your side. And we will protect you from any attacks by antisocial goons and communists.'

'Why, thank you, Sahib. I cannot tell you how happy it makes me feel to know that I can count on your friendship and support.'

Ambassador Burford walked towards his helicopter with President Sahib at his elbow. Both of them chatting amicably about cricket which neither one knew how to play but both professed to like.

Ambassador Burford stepped into his machine and waved good-bye. The ladder was retracted, the door closed, and then with an eardrum battering roar the machine rose on a swirling column of air and soon vanished into the pale blue sky.

President Sahib breathed a sigh of relief and decided to walk around the compound in order to inspect his domain. He checked the urine of his water-buffaloes to see if the color was healthy, exchanged ribald pleasantries with the talking parrots and made sure his pack of mongrels had been given their daily ration of powdered milk and bread. Having done all this, he returned to his rooms, rolled out his prayer mat and prayed earnestly, thanking Allah for being so good to him.

Then he fell fast asleep...

How long he slept is difficult to say. A week? A month? A year? Who can tell? Time in Pakypoor did not flow like a clear-water stream the way it does in other countries. In Pakypoor, Time stands still like a stagnant pool.

It must have been the noise of the crowd that finally woke him up. His heart knocking crazily in his chest, he sat straight up in bed, wondering what could have gone wrong. It sounded as though hundreds, no, thousands of people had surrounded the Government House compound and were howling like blood-thirsty wolves.

He hurried to find his slippers and cried out: 'Begum, begum, w-what's the matter? What is going on, for Allah's sake?'

Just then the old Begum burst into the room. Tears coursed down her wrinkled cheeks and her snow-white hair hung all awry in her face and eyes.

'*La hawl*, Salman's father,' she sputtered, wringing her hands in a classic gesture of despair. 'Something terrible has happened. Our rivers have disappeared. The five rivers of the Punjab—vanished—poof! Just like that. Gone—all gone, I'm telling you. The Beas, the Sutlej, the Ravi, the Chenab, even the mighty Jhelum—all of them drained dry! And a mob is at the door now, howling for your blood.'

'But Begum...'

'Don't Begum me now, you chuckleheaded fool,' the Begum expostulated. 'We are done for. I told you not to listen to that Barfloo.'

President Sahib stumbled to a window and peeked out. A sea of heads, some turbaned, some covered with scruffy black hair, some bald—an ocean of brown faces twisted in hideous grimaces of hate—a veritable forest of skinny arms waving placards and banners stretched as far as the eye could see. Many in the crowd wielded pitchforks, axes, knives, hatchets and home-made spears. Others had armed themselves with steel rods, lengths of iron pipe, chains and sections of metal fences. And they were all chanting in unison: 'Death to President Sahib! Death to those who stole our rivers!'

President Sahib drew back from the window in alarm. He was shaking like a eucalyptus leaf in a fresh breeze.

'What is the matter with these idiots?' he wondered aloud. 'I'll teach them a lesson they will never forget. I'll call General Yahoo Khan and tell him to shoot them all. Just imagine, after all the wonderful things I have done for them—is this the gratitude I get? What the hell do they want?'

'They want water,' said the Begum Sahiba.

'But I gave them sugar-sweet soda....'

'For the crops and fields, you idiot.'

'Get me General Yahoo...'

'He has gone over to their side. Don't you see, you simpleton? Yahoo knows that this is his big chance to gain the people's favor, overthrow you and take over power.'

'How dare he contemplate such treachery? My own Yahoo, the one I raised by hand, fed at my own table. How dare he?'

'Look, look,' said the old Begum. 'There he is, standing on top of the chromium-plated tank, the same one that you gave him on his birthday last year. There he is, right in front of the gate. What will we do? What will we do?'

The Begum moaned in bitter agony and wrung her hands some more. She had an irritating habit of repeating everything twice whenever a fit of anxiety came upon her.

Sure enough, right outside the magnificent wrought iron gates of the Government House, General Yahoo Khan stood on top of his shiny new tank which sparkled in the sunlight. His left hand was on his hip and with his right he held an electronic megaphone in front of his mouth. As he spoke, his clipped, army-style rhetoric rang out loud and metallic over the assembled throng:

'Listen to me, brothers. A great disaster has befallen us. Our rivers have been stolen. It appears that all five great rivers of the Punjab have vanished completely. We looked for them high and low, east and west. We even searched the Land-of-the-Infidels to the south, thinking that perhaps those spineless idol-worshippers had stolen them. But this was not the case. Now, by the grace of Allah, we have found out who took our rivers. People of Pakypoor, listen to me. Let me tell you what has happened. Your rivers have been sucked dry by the soda-water companies established by the Americans! The Yankee soda-water companies diverted them all into their giant bottling plants and now there is no water left for your fields and crops. It is obvious that President Sahib has sold our rivers.'

'What is he talking about?' said President Sahib. 'Why is he raving like a lunatic?'

'Don't you see, you senile dolt? All this is Barfood's handiwork. His soda-water factories have sucked the rivers dry.'

'B-b-but that is absurd,' stuttered the President. 'How could a few soda-water factories use up the water of five huge rivers?'

'A few, Salman's father, a few?' shrieked the old Begum, now succumbing totally to hysteria. 'Don't you know that they built hundreds of, thousands of bottling plants all over Pakypoor—millions of them...'

'Allah, Allah,' moaned President Sahib, clutching his head in both hands. 'What have I done?' he moaned. 'What will become of me?'

In the distance, he could clearly hear the voice of his erstwhile favorite General booming over the crowd, and each word sank into his heart like a poisoned dart.

'...this evil that has come to us is the direct result of President Sahib's actions. He has behaved like a cheap dancing-girl in front of the foreigners. He has committed vile and filthy acts for the sake of a few dollars. It is he who must be held responsible for the loss of the rivers. It is he who permitted the Americans to build these bottling plants. He is getting too old to be the Head of State. His mind is dull and befuddled. He has become quite senile. In fact, it is clear to all those who are close to him that he is completely mad. No doubt a mosquito has crawled up his nose and eaten away his brain. As you know, this is what happened to the Great Emperor Nimrood who also thought he was invincible. It is a miracle from Allah. Once again, He has used a tiny gnat to rid us of this tyrant and his greedy clan which has drained the wealth of our country for so many years. The hour has come at last to...'

By now President Sahib had begun to foam at the mouth. 'Why, that m-m-mother-sucking son of a whoremonger,' he stuttered, beside himself with anger.

He limped painfully to an ancient armoire, pulled out a rusty sword and started to lurch about the room, yelling and shouting and waving his weapon wildly.

The Begum, much alarmed by his behavior, cried out for his ADCs. 'Fazaldeen! Faltoo! Come here instantly.'

By now President Sahib was screaming incomprehensible gibberish and mingled curses with such ferocity that the veins on his neck swelled up like balloons and his eyes rolled back completely in his head until only the whites showed. In a maniacal frenzy, he slashed and hacked at the curtains and the stuffed chairs. Soon morsels of cotton wool and shreds of muslin hung in the air like snowflakes.

'*Hai Allah,*' the Begum cried, 'surely some evil jinn or demonic spirit has taken possession of him.'

At this point Fazaldeen and Faltoo rushed into the room and stared with shocked eyes at the ruination they saw all around.

'Fazaldeen, Faltoo, restrain him before he comes to harm. Obviously he is no longer himself.'

The ADCs also realized that President Sahib had lost touch with reality. They exchanged quick glances and then they made a running tackle, toppling President Sahib backwards and pinning him to the carpet with their combined weight. Then, while Fazaldeen held him down forcibly, Faltoo wrested the sword from his hand. The old man still had the strength of ten lesser men in him and he struggled furiously to get free, heaping vile abuse upon his ADCs all the while. But they hung on doggedly. They were still holding him spread-eagled on the floor like a toad ready for dissection when General Yahoo Khan burst into the room, megaphone in hand, and began giving orders. He spoke through his instrument as though he were still addressing a huge crowd. Apparently he relished the way the megaphone amplified his voice, gave it a certain gigantic authority and made him seem bigger than he was.

'Ho Faltoo,' he said in booming tones that commanded instant obedience. 'Handcuff this old man for his own safety and take him to the mental hospital right away.'

The old Begum let loose a blood-curdling shriek and backed into a corner beating her head and her chest with her hands. Her mouth opened and closed spasmodically as she strove to formulate words but not a sound emerged from her throat.

'*Jao, jao*,' Yahoo Khan said to her in a thunderous voice. 'Go look after your husband. You have no more business here. And you, Fazaldeen, take the presidential Cadillac and bring back Ambassador Barfood. Hurry! Only he can help us get back our vanished rivers.'

Berlin Danse Macabre

Okay, so it's 1939 again...

And Rula is dancing tonight at the White Mouse on the Kurfurstendamm. She performs like this every night, unless, of course, she is ill from lack of sleep or too much wine and cocaine, or too drained by traumas that test the tensile strength of her nerves. On a tiny stage, engulfed in clouds of cigar-smoke, she jerks and twitches in time to jazzy tunes until her limbs look like cursive hieroglyphs. Her eyes, blue as the Baltic and as cold, are indifferent to applause or derision. Her features are grossly sensual, with raw, red lips and blackened eye-lids. She flails her arms in parabolas and kicks extravagantly. Her legs, sheathed in smoked silk stockings have a castrating strength implicit in the muscled curve of the thigh, legs that gleam like oiled gun-metal under the klieg lights as she knifes the air with stiletto heels defining bright arcs in front of decrepit voyeurs and fetishists in the front row—Old Ludendorff's Prussian generals impotent since the action at Paschendaele, Civil Service relics left over from the Weimar Republic, National Socialists tumescent from lycanthropic lusts, and porcine Third Reich apparatchiki, all breathing hard through bureaucratic emphysemas, hoping for pornographic dreams and splendid nocturnal emissions in the cold Nazified nights to follow...

They feed on Rula's vitality like so many vampires, as she moves through tortured Republikan choreographies, expressing political ideas instead of musical ones, as she dances under the delusion that she is dancing on the grave of the Hohenzollerns.

In those days Fritz was also under her spell. But he preferred to hang back shyly in the shadows, pretending to be a camera. This happened so long ago. He was young then and couldn't resist conceiving an obsessive passion for this 'stripteuse' who personified all his private aberrations and those of the German body politic. Now, almost forty years later, Rula still dances through his brain as he sits alone and paralyzed in his wheelchair, staring out the window of his Brooklyn apartment. All he can see through cataract-weakened eyes is a ruined landscape, with gutted, fire-charred buildings and smoke rising from burnt-out hulks which remind him of Berlin after the war. At night the rats keep him awake with their chittering and scurrying under the floorboards. He knows they'll attack if he relaxes his vigil. He has festering bite-marks on his legs to prove what they can do. That's why he keeps the TV on all the time. It helps him to stay awake and he likes to talk to the people who flash by on the screen. Once a week, old Mrs Grobnik, a social worker of sorts, comes with a sack of groceries. She is horribly over-weight, reeks of gin and blows cigarette smoke at him through her mustache.

Every week he begs her to mail the letters he has written, but she tells him to hush up and stop bothering her. The unmailed letters pile up on the kitchen table in a dusty heap.

'Alla dem is dead,' Mrs Grobnik tells him. 'Dose pipple you wanna sen' letters. Alla dem cooked up in da hovens.'

Even so, Fritz has an acute need to communicate, to talk about what he has seen, especially now that Brooklyn is beginning to look like Berlin.

'No!' he shouts at the TV. 'The Nazi's...not here, not here.'

He touches the cold metal of his wheelchair with shaking hands and moves away from the window. Why can't he feel secure? He looks up at the ceiling, towards the heavens, the customary locus of a deity. But all he sees is a big yellow stain from some dire leakage upstairs, which is getting bigger and bigger. Bits of soggy plaster fall about him and an ammoniac stench ravages his nasal membranes. Will the ceiling cave in one of these days? Will a flood of piss and shit engulf his tiny world?

'It cannot happen here,' he murmurs to himself.

'How can you be sure?' say the Inner Voices.

'Well, because...,' Fritz gropes for words.

The Inner Voices snicker.

Almost every night there is a news report on TV about Nazis marching in some big city: Detroit, Chicago, Los Angeles. And now Brooklyn has taken on the look of Berlin—a wilderness of ruins stretching to the horizon with crumbling tenements, vandalized shops and streets filled with rubble. In cracked shop-windows naked manikins stand in attitudes of surprise, water drips from leaky fire-hydrants and thin mongrels root in the litter...

Fritz looks on passively. The metamorphosis he had desired has finally taken place. He has become a camera. He had longed for this transformation through all those years that he worked as camera-man for UFA studios. He is merely an open eye, looking upon the world from behind protective filters designed to admit only the flowing chiaroscuro—diffractions of light, incidental beams, flickering shadows, images that fade, dissolve and flutter away like tenuous ghosts in an expressionistic montage.

Most of the time he feels like an alien, an auslander, and constantly thinks about leaving Germany. But so far he has not been able to make up his mind even though all the auguries, the omens—squadrons of black Hapsburg eagles in the sky, the colors of the entrails of sacrificed victims—all indicate that the time of exodus, of exile is at hand.

He looks to Albert-the-Genius for advice but Albert won't say anything. He is too dazzled by deliriums of light and the higher mathematic to be of any help to a simple camera-man. The relativity of Time and Space, the unconscionable weight of sunbeams, has addled Albert's brain. He is too much in love with his brand new laboratory, designed especially for him by Mendelssohn in the new Expressionistic style. It sits on the ground like a potato with windows—an organic shape. Is there anything more organic than a potato? It looks like a brown tuber that has just emerged from the earth and is still half buried. The lines of the silhouette are flowing, curvilinear. The facade is an uneven expanse of nubby grey, texturized plaster punctured with a number of odd-shaped apertures that function as windows.

One afternoon (by now it was already getting too late and Jews had begun to disappear off the streets of Berlin with a disturbing regularity), Fritz went to see Albert. He saw him sitting at his desk considering the declensions of light, trying to prepare himself psychologically for the sunset developing slowly over Germany. A keening wind shredded and dispersed the last of the rain clouds, and warm saffron beams slanted in past the mullions to stain the mahogany desk-top, the crystal paper-weight, the virgin sheets of paper, and the Kerman on the floor with washes of palest apricot and peach.

Albert was fascinated, one might even say obsessed with light, the way it fell through filtering layers of ozone, the way it bent in deference to the ponderous gravity of celestial bodies, the way it diffused, scattered and illumined the world of objects and the dark recesses of the mind—light that worked on the heart like music, evoking joy, hope, sadness or modulated into fugues of transiency and impending departures, light that faded even as he sat solving equations, light that degenerated at last to colors of the holocaust, going from flaming orange to a curdled mauve and finally fusing with the deep indigo and blackness of night itself... .

Fritz stepped quietly back out of the room and came away without saying a word.

Meanwhile...well, here we are in downtown Berlin and Fritz is at his usual post at the White Mouse, hoping that if he drinks enough brandy he may get up the courage to declare his passion to Rula. But Rula is too absorbed in her own sensual frenzy and too interested in the customers in the front row who spend big bucks at the club. The little round tables and cane-back chairs in the front have been taken up by members and guardians of the *ancien regime*, Wilhelm II's kith and kin, led by one Prince Chlodwig zu Hohenlohe-Schillingsfurst, their acknowledged leader. Chlodwig's mentality can be gauged by the fact that he once declared in front of newspaper reporters that he thought Hauptmann's plays were idiotic. Then there is Chlodwig's passion for Rula, much bruited by tabloids like *Vossische Zeitung* and a scandal in all the spas from Baden-Baden to Alexisbad.

Chlodwig leans his monocled face towards Adolfus and whispers something. All the regular patrons of the White Mouse know what is going on between Chlod, Adolfus and Rula. Adolfus, apparently, has a cocaine connection in Maracaibo. Rula likes the stuff but doesn't have the cash to pay for it. Chlodwig has the money and he has made it plain to Rula that she can have all the wonderful white powder she wants provided she participates in the orgies that he likes to stage modelled after the ones described in *Venus in Furs*, his most favorite work written by his buddy, Count Sacher von Masoch. Amazingly enough, Rula has been turning down these invitations so far. But Adolphus has started to give her small doses of the white powder free of charge, just enough to sustain her habit. Soon he will stop. Then Prince Chlodwig zu Hohenlohe-Schillingsfurst will....

The minions of Kaiser Wilhelm II (Fritz calls them 'Wilhelminions') have been spending more and more time around the White Mouse lately. They are easy to spot in their tight, four button jackets with wide lapels, baggy pants and, of course, snap-brim fedoras. They affect the look of the Chicago Mob and self-consciously cultivate the snarl sinister, the riposte malicious, and the cruelty gratuitous. Most of them are from Prussia. But recently, a few smarmy Latin types with dark, oily skins and pencil-line mustaches have begun to show up. Agents of Mussolini, no doubt, or of Franco. So far they've just been watching and waiting. They strike menacing poses and fondle their roscoes suggestively in front of the hat-check girls. These are pressure tactics. Soon, soon they'll move in and demand a cut of the take.

Fritz knows most of them quite well from his days at UFA studios, before the inflationzeit killed Berlin's movie industry. These fellows worked as extras in the third-grade monster movies then in vogue, wonderfully at home amidst the sets designed to induce horror. Decked out in black capes, they enjoyed baring their fangs to thrill the underlings from the slums of Charlottenburg and Pankow. But now that the final scenes of Nosferatu have been filmed, they have no place to go. They long for that vampire ambience. O the terrible *schadenfreude*, as you crawl about in crepescular fogs snarled between sooted-brick chimneys, or the grave-stones crumbled into a fungoid necropolis, looking for blood meals at the blackest hour of night...

Nowadays they have little to do. Their lives lack direction. So they gather for patriotic rallies, sing rousing choruses of 'Deutschland Uber Alles' and listen to orators who lecture them on such concepts as *Lebensraum* and the pan-Germanic *geist.*

Each Wilhelminion thinks he is an Ubermensch. Late at night they prowl up and down Tauenzien or Friederichstrasse, to prey on schoolboys who are weak from hunger and will usually agree to any sexual perversity—oral, anal or manual—for a decent meal or a few marks.

And as if all this weren't enough, runners have been coming to Fritz with more alarming news. The Teutonic wolves, it seems, have broken out of their pens in the Tiergarten zoo and are headed down the Unter den Linden towards the Reich Chancellary. And as they march, they sing:

> And Rathenau, old Walther,
> Shall have a timely halter.

Yes, they are musical, these wolves, and have quite a repertoire of anti-Jewish ditties. Soon they will regroup by the Brandenburg Tor, then fan out all over the city, first in small packs, crowding into local *bierhalles* and *wein-kellars*. Then they'll mass in huge assemblies at the *sport-palast* and the hippodrome. And when their brothers hear the rallying cry, more of them will come loping out of the fens and bogs of Pomerania, across the Flaming fault, and over the Luneburg heath. They will multiply, divide, and spread across Hesse, Thuringia and the terminal morraines that reach into the Schwarzwald. Soon all of Germany will echo as they howl in ecstacy and hunt for human flesh in towns and cities.

Ah! Berlin... Berlin. City of love and pain. City of discord. City of hate. City of memories... .

Fritz said to Albert: Something bad is about to happen.

Fritz said: I have seen the signs—clouds shaped like swastikas at sundown and at night, floating above the canal like tattered wisps of grey brume, the ghosts of Karl Liebkneckt and Rosa Luxemburg.

He swears Rosa is trying to reach him from beyond the grave. She wants to tell him something. But it is difficult for her to communicate across inter-galactic space and time. Rosa, Rosa, my sweet summer rose, where are your budded beauties? Rose of Masuria, so devoted to the cause of the people, so courageous. Even in prison, even in the deepest dungeon they couldn't kill your love for life. From her cell she wrote how she longed '...to be free and stroll about the fields or even only in the streets, to make a halt before every garden during April-May, to gaze at the verdant bushes, observing how budding leaves are turned differently in the case of each of them, how the maple tree strews its greenish-yellow stars, how the first speedwell peeps forth from under the grass...'

But no, the Wilhelminions wouldn't let her live. Couldn't let her live. By 1919 the spirit of Attila had begun to roar for a blood offering, preferably the blood of a communist, better yet, a Jewish communist. And Rosa, did your dark eyes, already bleak with suffering, plead for mercy when the

Wilehlminions raised their knives, or did you quietly offer your neck like Isaac? Thine is the sacrifice, O Lord God of the Hosts, Thine the knife and Thine the victim. Let Thy will be done. Amen.

Yes, it is written in all the secular histories that they beat her up brutally, mutilated her body and dumped it in the Landwehrkanal to be devoured by blue-eyed Hapsburg crocodiles.

Rula, bathed in sweat by now, is into her final, her terminal gyrations. On an evening exactly like this, back in 1922, right here at the White Mouse, Fritz discovered the assassination plot against the Foreign Minister, Walther Rathenau, the scion of a prominent Jewish family.

Fritz is in the shadows looking on passively. Two over-dressed women, come wriggling and sqirming in between the tables and chairs, tripping over feet, falling into the laps of businessmen and getting their butts slapped by jovial drunks as they look for a place to sit. They squeal and giggle in high-pitched voices, pretending to be very upset. As they settle down on the banquette next to Fritz, he realizes that they are a couple of guys in drag, in fact, Zwerge and Mucke, two hairdressers who used to work for the studios. They wear expensive silk dresses and carry fur wraps (purchased at Wertheim's most likely). Obviously they were making more money as transvestites and were having a good time doing it. Fritz leans back, hoping they won't see him. Luckily, They don't. They are too busy whispering to each other, bewigged heads close together. Fritz tries to concentrate on the dancing, but during lulls in the music he picks up snatches of their conversation.

'... Rathenau...'

'... in his house...'

'... are you mad? Guards, servants...'

'... street then...Konigsallee.'

'...ambush...'

Fritz can hardly believe what he has begun to suspect. It looks like the two are talking about the Foreign Minister,

Walter Rathenau. Is this some kind of assassination plot? Perhaps he should do something, jump up and accuse these two of conspiring to kill a high government official or run to the police. But he doesn't move. The old Camera-man Syndrome has him in an iron grip, the mode of existence learned at UFA and there cultivated and developed to perfection. He finds he cannot stir. The camera is a passive observer. It cannot step in to save the Hero or Heroine. It cannot participate in the story or influence events. It only records what the Almighty Director wishes to record.

Zwerg and Mucke raise their glasses towards Prince Chlodwig in a champagne salute. The Prince smiles and nods amiably. Then he notices one of Rula's pubic hairs in his drink. (She really has been jumping about quite a bit.) He picks it out and holds it up for all to see—a light-brown crinkled strand with a golden drop of champagne still clinging to it. Yes, Chlod, you rascal you, doesn't this remind you of another scenario in which Rula lets you drink a yellow liquid in the privacy of her dressing room, dribbling straight from the source?

Deep within the cogged mechanisms of his heart, Fritz knows that if the Wilhelminions want to destroy Rathenau, no one can stop them. It's really high time he left The White Mouse. The cabaret is getting more sinister, more political. But for some reason he cannot bring himself to leave, not while Rula is still dancing. He is such an incurable romantic. He believes in love as a Force, a Power. He is a diseased dreamer of the old school, the school of Goethe, Lessing and Herder, haunted by vague, mystical yearnings, a need to transcend his meagre physical self, rise above the *burgerlich* circumventions, lose himself in foggy, alpine meadows and discard his tainted mortality. He thinks of his love for Rula as a Grand Passion. No adolescent infatuation this, but the kind of love-affair that used to unfold in the discreet lobbies of turn-of-the-century hotels all ruby-red velvet and crystal chandeliers—love born out of a *fin-de-siécle* urgency, with fatigue and desire held in even balance,

evolving through Proustian nuances towards guilt...love
sharpened to a keen, cutting edge by protocols that
demanded restraint and secrecy and, of course, Wagnerian
arias in the background, perhaps the overture from Tristan
and Isolde, soaring upwards in stupendous diapasons of
harmony that inspire and exalt, lift the soul to ethereal
heights...

But Rula doesn't give a tinker's curse for Fritz. She prefers
to hang around with homosexuals, the languid Ganymedes
who frequent the El Dorado at 28, Martin Lutherstrasse,
men who have been emasculated by the Weimar economy
or by their own perverse needs.

Then one day—June 24, 1922—it happened. While Fritz
and Albert and all the others like them were waiting around
flat-footed, wondering if the murky morning of the *Republik*
would mature into a brighter afternoon, it happened.

Now, many years later, Fritz cannot figure out if he simply
imagined the event or read about it in the *Vossiche Zeitung*
which printed the account of one Krischbin, the bricklayer.
Or did he actually see the whole action? Even if he did, he is
not about to admit this for political reasons.

Anyway, here we go...Lights! Camera! Action!

It is a stifling day. The sky heated to incandescence, glows
a sulphurous yellow. A day for an open touring car, just like
the one coming down the Konigsallee now, a long, powerful
tourer with the top down and two men dressed in leather
coats, helmets and goggles sitting in the back. The tourer
overtakes the smaller car, swerves in front and forces it to a
screeching stop. A distinguished-looking man dressed in a
business suit, sitting in the smaller car, looks up in alarm.
One of the leather-coated goons props the butt of his
automatic weapon against his shoulder and fires into the
back of the car from a point-blank range. The man clutches
at his throat with an expression of pain and falls backwards.
There is another rapid burst from the weapon. His chauffeur
jumps out shouting for help and runs down the street. The
man at the wheel of the tourer takes a hand-grenade, pulls

the pin and tosses it into the small car. As they pull away with a roar, the grenade explodes. The body in the back seat of the small car thrusts violently upward, shredded by metal fragments and the vehicle shudders on its springs, a smoking, ruined shell...

'No!' Fritz shouts, making an effort to wake up from this historical nightmare. But the sound of the explosion that he heard is very real. Flames and smoke appear on the Brooklyn skyline. A leaky gas main and a careless cigarette tossed by a vagrant is all it takes.

Fritz moans in a muffled voice. He has fallen out of his chair and his useless legs are crumpled beneath him awkwardly. He does not have the strength to pull himself back up. In the darkness, his groping fingers encounter something sticky and wet. Is it blood? Yes, it is. The rats have been nibbling at his legs again, reopening old wounds. They watch and wait for him to fall asleep. Then they emerge from their holes, from behind the wainscoting and start chewing on his legs. It is getting harder and harder for him to stay alert.

Walter Rathenau was given a grand state funeral. They laid out his body in the Chamber of the Reichstag, draped the coffin in the colors of the *Republik*—Black. Red. Gold. And there was music in the background. Hark! Yes, it is Siegfried's funeral march from Gotterdeämmerung.

But for Fritz there won't be such pomp. By now the rats are everywhere. In the White Mouse. In the White House. I must get a cat. Rula is dancing with a white mouse in the white house. Albert, Albert, what have your mathematical equations proved? Are we in Brooklyn or is this Berlin? No, no this is Berklyn! Dance, Rula, dance. The rats will eat the cat. In the end...nothing.

In Martha's Vineyard there are Many Bruised and Broken Fruits

The trip to Martha's Vineyard was the wife's idea. The thought of spending yet another day poking around garish shops cluttered with tourist trinkets held little appeal for me. I would have preferred a leisurely lunch and several steins of Sam Adams' peerless ale in some cozy pub in Hyannis Port. But the spouse decreed that we must see Martha's Vineyard. And whatsoever the spouse decrees, so...

As it was, we barely made it to the ferry in time. We'd been bickering all morning—not over anything significant, nor with any real passion. But too much togetherness had begun to take its toll. After several days of travel, of bad but expensive meals and flimsy mattresses ripe with mildew, we'd reached a threshold of irritability, a flashpoint of nerves that sparked into arguments at every minor inconvenience.

By the time we arrived at Woods Hole, the sky over the harbor was the color of freshly-poured concrete. The damp air held a threat of rain and out beyond the docks and derricks, a dark ocean heaved sluggishly like used motor oil. We purchased our tickets and sprinted up the boarding ramp.

* * *

The ferry boat shuddered as the engines started up. The rumble of the massive diesel motors resonated inside the hull, came up my legs and made my knees feel weak. Watch your step, the vessel seemed to say, tread on me with care. Trembling like a highstrung race horse at the starting gate, the big boat tugged at the thick hawsers as if eager to get going.

The growl of the engines changed to a full-throated roar and with a loud blast from the fog horn, the ferry slowly moved out of the harbor, making a foamy wake of old Irish lace as it gained speed. A squadron of seagulls flew alongside, mewing like hungry kittens and a misty, grey light drizzled down out of a low bank of clouds.

I made my way to the foredeck and stood there for a while to savor the fresh breeze. Suddenly a hubbub of voices towards the rear of the vessel attracted my attention. A small crowd had formed at the railing and people were pointing and gesturing excitedly. I hurried over to find out the cause of all this commotion. A child's doll, it appeared, had fallen overboard. I caught a glimpse of the toy as it swept past us on the steely surface of the water, a Raggedy Anne with staring eyes, flaming hair and red manacled socks. Some child had flung it in anger or let it drop accidentally. The incident caused a stir and people chattered about it for a long time.

The crowd of vacationers and tourists milled about the ferry boat in a festive mood. But as I stared at the faces in the crowd, I noticed something odd. Some of the people, rather a large number, in fact, didn't look quite right.

At first, I couldn't identify the quality or feature that made them different, made them stand out in this indefinable way. Was it something about their eyes, or their facial expressions or their mode of dress? I couldn't put my finger on any one factor.

There were no physical deformities or disfiguring marks to set these folks apart. They wore the same kinds of T-shirts and jeans and parkas and jogging shoes as the other tourists. And yet, I couldn't get rid of the sensation that amidst our cheerful holiday throng were people who were not quite...well—right.

I decided to examine them more closely. The survey confirmed my initial impression. With a mild shock, I realized that we had on board a large contingent of mental patients. They must have belonged to some local hospital or institution. And this excursion to Martha's Vineyard must have been arranged for them as a kind of therapy.

It was charming, even heartbreaking, to see these 'mentally handicapped' types doing their best to blend in with the other passengers. Not wishing to stand out or be noticed, they tried hard to make themselves inconspicuous. If they had any abnormal mannerisms or tendencies, they held them under firm control. In fact, I had to look carefully to single out one of them from amidst the other passengers. Nevertheless, they couldn't escape my attention and I made a game of spotting them.

I would scan a bench crowded with passengers until I found one. Then I'd stare and stare at this individual who would be trying hard to stay composed and nonchalant. But my intense, probing scrutiny would melt the cool demeanor of my victim, a kind of panic would set in and hands and feet would begin to move uncontrollably. Finally, unable to be still, the poor creature would get up and scurry away.

Surely, this game had a sadistic side. But sadism comes easy when you get to be a certain age and are filled with odd desires and frustration. To keep boredom at bay, I decided to study these individuals more closely.

There was 'the jock,' for instance, a sturdy, young fellow whose polyester polo shirt was several sizes too small for him and accentuated his well-developed biceps. He could have passed for a college athlete, but his mouth hung open loosely and his eyes had a vacant look.

There was 'Captain Ahab,' a plump, man with a great, bald, dome of a head and a ragged, grey-streaked beard. He had a huge stomach and his pudgy body exhibited a general lack of muscle tone. He could have passed as an eccentric leftover from the 'hippie' era. What betrayed him was his new, white dress shirt which still retained all the creases from the way it had been packaged. His keepers had bought it especially for the excursion, but no one had taken the trouble to iron it. He'd cinched his pants high up on his waist almost under his armpits in fact, and they enveloped his posterior as though it were a sack of potatoes.

Whatever his IQ, 'Captain Ahab' appeared to be a happy man. He smiled constantly—at his fellow passengers, at the seagulls, at the clouds, at the blue plastic chairs.

Then there was 'Sparkles,' a rather dainty, young girl whose agitated manner made her stand out.

She had a creamy complexion as if she had spent all her life indoors and her large, intelligent brown eyes seemed to look on everything and everyone with the cautious air of a paranoid personality. But it was the headband she wore to control her mass of unruly, reddish-brown hair, that betrayed her. The spouse noticed it first and made some snarky remark. Encrusted with glittering sequins and almost three inches wide, the headband did not go with the bleached blue denim jacket and gray corduroy skirt she had on. Obviously an impulse purchase, it looked more like a bandage for a head wound than an ornamental accessory.

'Sparkles' could not sit down due to some uncontrollable mental or physical impetus. She roamed all over the ferry boat restlessly, with a can of coke in one hand and a cigarette in the other.

At first, she had me fooled. I thought of her as just a flower-child left over from another era, someone who had not given up the dreams of 'Free Love, Flowers and Peace.' But what gave her away finally, was the way she talked to herself.

Every time she went past me on one of her circular jaunts around the ferry boat, she'd be mumbling to herself and waving her cigarette.

There were others: older women with dense mustaches and bad teeth; men with scruffy hair and exceedingly narrow faces who sat clutching paperbacks. When I stared at them they instinctively looked away.

On an irrational impulse, I decided to approach 'Sparkles,' to see if I could get close to the personality behind those gentle eyes.

Her gay headband proclaimed her as a free spirit. I wondered if she'd respond to male attention. She seemed rather vain and self-conscious, someone with a keen sense of herself as an object of desire.

When I saw 'Sparkles' head for the cafeteria, I mumbled something about wanting a coke to the spouse and followed her.

A discord of voices bounced and echoed within the steel interior of the cafeteria. People clamored against a counter, waving their money at harried attendants. 'Sparkles' stood outside this mêlée, hesitant, nervous.

I edged up close behind her, near enough to catch the flowery odor of her shampoo. She glanced back, recognized me as someone who had been staring at her, and then quickly looked away.

'Would you like something?' I asked.

She made no response, but I could sense that she'd heard me.

'How about a coke?' I said, as casually as if she were an old acquaintance.

She looked around the room as if searching for someone, then rolled her eyes in a dramatic gesture of surrender.

'Get me one,' she said abruptly, as though she were giving an order and thrust a crumpled bill at me.

'Keep it,' I said, and moved towards the counter, elbowing several people aside roughly. I bought two cans of coke and returned, bearing one in each fist, like hunting trophies.

'Sparkles' had retreated to a corner of the room.

I handed her a can, opened the other and took a long swig.

'Ugh,' I said. 'I don't think this is very cold.'

'Sparkles' held her can of coke with a guilty air, as if dubious about accepting something from a stranger.

'Go ahead, drink up,' I told her, 'before it gets any warmer.'

She shrugged and opened the can.

'I should thank you, I suppose,' she said.

Her voice and accent surprised me. She spoke in resonant, well-modulated tones as though she had trained for a career on stage.

'That's okay,' I said, trying to muster enough courage to ask her name. After a moment or two of awkward silence, I decided to be brave.

'What's your name?' I said.

Again she looked away and did not answer. I got the feeling she seemed to have a fear of being seen talking to me for some reason. Her anxiety matched mine. I really did not want the spouse seeing me talking to her. I would have to explain, find excuses.

'I'm Jay,' I said.

'Cindy,' she said finally, taking quick, short drags on a stub. 'I'm Cindy.'

'Short for Cinderella, right?' I said, grinning at her.

She flashed a quick, nervous smile and shook her head. The spangles and sequins on her headband glittered like diamonds in a tiara and seemed to light up the drab cafeteria.

Suddenly, the loud clamor of the tourists died away and we were in a stately ballroom with a gleaming floor and walls covered with rich tapestries of silk and velvet. Cinderella stood before me in a flowing gown of pink chiffon. The band struck up a waltz. I swept her up in my arms and waltzed away, lightly and smoothly, across gleaming marble, beneath a bright milky way of chandeliers. Her glass shoes, fashioned from purest crystal, struck sparks as we swung around and the applause of lords and ladies washed over us like the music of distant wind-chimes.

'Let's go below,' I said to her, 'it's quieter down there.'

She gazed at the floor, possibly weighing her response. In an attempt to encourage her, I pushed my way through the crowd and headed down a flight of metal stairs. As I clattered down into the cabin below, I sensed that she was right behind me.

I don't know what I had in mind. Nothing very sensible or serious, I'm sure. Something in the way of amusement, perhaps, a game....

I led the way down into a dimly-lit cabin filled with odors of rust, mildew and damp sea-salt. The racket from the engines echoed loudly in here. One could almost hear the wheels turning, the gears meshing, and the drive shafts whirring. A few elderly passengers huddled on wooden benches ranged along the walls, but they paid no attention when we entered. In a far corner, a fat steel pipe or tube of some kind came down out of the low ceiling and went into the metal floor. I sauntered over and leaned against it.

As we stood there, she began to fumble in her suede bag for a pack of cigarettes and went through an elaborate ritual of removing one and putting it between her lips. I noticed that her hands were shaking.

When she brought the matchbox out, I took it from her hands.

'Allow me,' I said. 'Though you really shouldn't smoke.'

'I know,' she said. 'I've tried to quit several times.'

'Where are you from?' I asked her.

'Why?' she said.

'Why what?' I asked.

'Why do you want to know?'

'Curiosity, I guess.'

'Curiosity killed the cat.'

'I'm not a cat.'

'You're sly as a cat.'

'Really?' I said, showing mock surprise.

'Sure.'

I got the feeling she was evading my questions. She obviously didn't want to admit too much. She sounded normal, quite intelligent, in fact, but she seemed unwilling to offer opinions. There was a certain gloomy moodiness about her which clearly marked her as someone with mental problems.

When she puffed on her cigarette, I was amazed to see how fragile and delicate her hand was. I could tell she'd never done any rough, manual work.

'You don't have to tell me anything,' I said to her. 'I didn't mean to pry.'

'Am I weird?' she asked. 'I guess I'm being really weird.'

'I just wanted to...you know, get to know you.'

'Ah, yes.' she said. 'That's a good one.'

'What do you mean?' I said, rather chagrined.

'Line,' she said, chuckling loudly. 'That's a good line.'

'Hey,' I said, with some heat, 'it's not a line. I mean that.'

She shook her head as if to clear her thoughts and put a hand on my arm.

'Look,' she said, 'I...I have mental problems. They...the doctors think I'm slow or something.'

I uttered a nervous bark of laughter, doing my best to hide the fact that I already suspected that.

'You seem pretty smart to me,' I said, gallantly.

'I get by,' she murmured, looking around in that furtive manner she had. 'I'm on medication—lots of kinds of pills.'

'Me too,' I told her, trying for solidarity. 'I can't sleep unless I take a couple of sleeping pills.'

'I know what you mean,' she said, seriously.

We talked like any two people who had just met, awkward, hesitant, unsure of the direction that the conversation ought to take.

I wanted to ask her personal questions, find out more about her.. But I could hear the steady thump of the pistons behind me—a reminder that we had very little time. What good would it have done me to delve into her biography?

I told her that the wife and I were visiting from California.

'I've always wanted to go there,' she said. 'Get away from stuffy, old Boston.'

'You'd be a hit on the beaches,' I told her.

'Would I?' she murmured looking into the smoke curling up from her cigarette.

'Sure.'

'The sea,' she said mysteriously, 'the sea is the mother of all life.'

'You look like a person who reads a lot,' I said.

'No,' she said. 'I can't concentrate on words, on the page...I lose interest. But I like to watch movies, especially old black and white ones.'

'Those are better than the new Hollywood trash.'

'You think so?'

'I'm positive.'

'You're not just saying this to agree with me?'

'I'm with you on this. Really.'

We talked some more, exchanging other inconsequential tidbits of information that tourists exchange with each other.

Then I said: 'I must get back on deck.'

'Don't go,' she said, quickly. 'Stay.'

This caught me by surprise. I hadn't thought she had any particularly strong desire to continue our conversation.

'Look, I enjoyed talking to you. But...my wife...she's probably thinking I fell overboard or something.'

'Please,' she said with a peculiar intensity in her voice, 'talk to me.'

She shot a furtive glance at the figures dozing on the benches and came and stood quite close to me until we were both sort of hidden behind the tube. Then she took my hand and pressed it against her chest.

'Feel me,' she commanded in a tense whisper. 'Feel me up.'

For a brief instant I was aware of the springy softness of her breasts beneath my fingers. But then I pulled back my hand quickly.

I realized I'd made a big blunder. The girl did have a loose screw.

'Later,' I said in a breezy, breathless manner as I backed away rapidly. 'See ya later.'

Waving my arms in a haphazard farewell, I raced up the stairs, taking them two at a time and soon emerged into the light and air of the top deck.

'Where were you?' said my wife. 'I've been looking for you all over this wretched boat.'

* * *

A heavy rain cut loose soon after we docked at Martha's Vineyard. As we debarked, I noticed 'Sparkles' and 'Jock' and 'Ahab' moving down the ramp along with their group, bumping into each other like cattle in a chute. 'Sparkles' did not look back and I did my best to stay away from her.

It rained most of the afternoon. The wife and I darted from one shop to the next, sloshing through countless puddles. I found myself wondering if I'd run into 'Sparkles' again and played out many scenarios of how I might make amends for running away from her so abruptly.

The touch of her fragile hand on mine still lingered in my memory and the image of those anxious, brown eyes looking up into mine.

By the time the ferry boat started back towards Woods Hole, the sea had become even more restless. Darkness had spread across the sky and a gale-force wind could be heard whistling through the rigging. The passengers gathered in the main cabin, looking bedraggled and weary.

I checked out the passengers and was rather pleased to see that the party of mental patients was returning with us. This meant that Cindy had to be on board. I wanted to locate her, talk to her again, just to make sure she wasn't hurt or angry, but at the back of my mind there still lurked a fear that she might say or do something odd or unusual. Telling my wife that I wanted a drink, I headed for the bar. I bought scotch on the rocks and threw it back quickly to lay down. Then I got a beer to quench a throat-burning thirst.

I drank the beer too fast and bought another one. But the booze didn't make things any sunnier.

After a while, I got bored with standing around and proceeded to the cabin below. The room was crowded with people. But in the far corner, a sparkle of sequins caught my eye. Cindy stood near the large tube, smoking meditatively. I pushed my way towards her through a mass of bodies. She looked at me with just a hint of a smile.

'Did you have a nice day?' I said.

'Wonderful,' she said. 'Had a wonderful time.'

Her eyes looked moist and red as though she had been crying.

'I want to talk you,' I said. 'Can we find someplace a bit quieter?'

'Dunno,' she said and shrugged.

'Come,' I said. 'Follow me.'

I grabbed her arm and led her out of the room as though I were saving her from a fate worse than death. I had a hunch that the bay where they parked the cars would be empty.

'Where are we going?' she asked.

'Down below,' I told her.

'Hell,' I heard her mutter.

I found the door which led down into the parking bay. A sign said: NO PASSENGERS ALLOWED. I turned the knob and pushed.

We were in a cavernous hold, in which they parked the cars and trucks. Weak bulbs held in little steel-mesh cages threw mustard-colored shadows along the walls. One could hear the sound of threshing propellers just below the steel floor. We were in the bowels of the boat where the stench of raw diesel blended nastily with the smell of stagnant sea water.

'Are we allowed in here?' Cindy wanted to know.

'Sure,' I said. 'Let's find a place to sit.'

I led the way down a narrow aisle which ran along the side. There was no place for us to sit anywhere so I began yanking on the door-handles of the vehicles. Eventually, the rear door of a beige sedan yielded.

'In here,' I said. 'Come on.'

Cindy hung back.

'It's okay,' I said.

'This one yours?' she asked.

I hesitated for a split-second, then the lie rolled off my tongue.

'Sure,' I said. 'Yes yes.'

Cindy stepped in and closed the door behind her.

'It's a nice car,' she said with great seriousness as she settled back and passed her hands sensuously over the brown velveteen upholstery.

'It is,' I agreed, savoring the snug ambiance.

'Look,' I said. 'I want to apologize for my behavior this morning.'

'Why?' she asked.

'Well, I left rather abruptly.'

'Why?' she said again.

'You mean, why did I run away?'

'Yes, why did you run away?'

'Well, I was worried...my wife, you see. She would have come looking and....'

'Don't worry,' she murmured, leaning back and closing her eyes. 'I can keep secrets.'

'I just didn't want to give the wrong impression....'

She opened her eyes and looked at me, a lopsided smile on her face. In the dim light inside the car, her headband glimmered like a distant constellation.

'You're dumb,' she said. 'Dumb but nice.'

'Gee, thanks for the compliment.'

'I wasn't born yesterday,' she said.

'But I'm older than you. I....'

She shook her head in the affirmative and once again went through the rigmarole of fumbling in her handbag for her pack of cigarettes, and lit up.

Inside the car with the windows rolled up, all the external rumbling sounded muffled and distant.

'I wish...I wish ...' I started a sentence not knowing where it would end. I could have said a great deal but a sense of futility came over me. An awkward silence held us in a painful embrace.

'Have you ever been to California?' I asked her.

'What?' she said as though she had not been listening to me.

'California. Have you ever been there?'

'In my mind,' she said. 'I've been there in my mind.'

She took a few quick puffs and stubbed out her cigarette in an ashtray in the padded door handle.

'You should go to L.A.' I said. 'It's your kind of place.'

'Yeah?' she said and leaned towards me.

Then out of the clear blue she said: 'Do you want me?'

The blunt abruptness of this question stunned me.

'What?'

'Do me,' she said, huskily. 'Do me now.'

She moved closer towards me.

I backed away from her, my pulse beginning to throb at my temples.

Beneath the sequins of her headband, her eyes glittered brightly..

'Look...I hardly know you.'

'It doesn't matter,' she said. 'Go ahead.'

Then, before I could make any kind of response, she grabbed my hand and pushed it up under her skirt, all the way to her crotch. I felt a hot, furry cavity against my fingers.

The blood rushed to my head and I yanked my hand back quickly as though it had been scalded.

'Whoa!' I muttered. 'Hold on a sec.'

She leaned towards me. I fumbled behind me for the door handle.

'Feel me up,' she said. 'Touch me.'

'Wait a minute,' I stuttered. 'I'm married. I can't...'

'Please,' she begged and grabbed my arm. 'Don't go.'

I pulled away from her, opened the door and stepped out.

'This is crazy,' I said. 'I didn't mean to...I didn't think...shit, not this.'

My hands were shaking.

'Let's go back,' I told her. 'Come on.'

'No,' she said sullenly and looked the other way.

'I'm sorry,' I said. 'All this is my fault.'

She hid her face in her hands and stubbornly moved her head from side to side.

'Let's go back,' I said.

Again she shook her head violently without looking up. I stood there for a few seconds, listening to the jumble of noises echoing eerily in the hold, wondering how I'd gotten myself into this situation.

'Okay,' I said. 'Suit yourself.'

I shut the car door firmly and walked quickly back up and locked myself in a stall in the Men's toilet. Tremors were going up and down my limbs and my heart thudded against my ribs like a trapped gerbil.

Self-loathing rose up within me in waves of nausea. A peculiar need always led me into lives where I had no right to be. It had happened before. Other chance meetings. Other failed connections. Each time it was a different girl, but the same longing. Something about big ships stirred my blood, made me thrash about in my chains.

Once, on the midnight run from Folkestone to Boulogne, I saw a girl sleeping on the carpeted floor of the cabin with her head on her knapsack. I watched and waited. But when she woke up she wandered off with some people.

Then on the ferry from Port Angeles to Victoria, I saw her again. She stood on the fore-deck all the way, with her face into the wind. In the light of the setting sun, her hair glittered like filaments of gold. She knew she looked good. But I did not speak to her.

Then, several years later, I saw her again. This time on the Thoreson-Townsend ferry-boat from Zeebrugge to

Dover. I bought her a beer and lit her cigarette. I was alone. Late that night, we found a Bed & Breakfast inn perched on the white cliffs of Dover. Next day she caught the express train to London.

After what seemed like a very long time, I emerged from the Men's Room and went looking for the spouse. I found her standing outside the bar.

'Have you been drinking?' she asked. 'I've been looking for you all over....'

'Bathroom,' I mumbled. 'Stomach trouble. Must have eaten something.'

'I told you not to eat those raw oysters.'

'Shouldn't have,' I said. 'Think I'll step out. Need fresh air.'

I opened a door and stepped out into a blast of wind and rain. The slippery deck heaved and tilted beneath my feet, making it hard to move in any direction. I wrapped my arms around a railing and just stood there, letting the raindrops peck away at my face.

Suddenly, I heard a kind of scream from the stern of the boat, followed by muffled shouts. The cries and yells could be heard clearly above the churning engines and the noise of crashing waves.

'Oh, God,' someone screamed. 'Do something.'

'What happened?' came another voice. 'What's going on?'

'Someone's fallen overboard.'

Even as I heard these words, the sound of the diesel engines died down abruptly and a siren set up a panicked whooping. Half a dozen searchlights came on and several of the men who operated the ferry ran towards quarterdeck.

Several others began to undo the straps of a big container on the foredeck which held the rubber raft.

'Man overboard,' shouted one of the sailors.

'It's not a man,' someone else cried out. 'It's a woman.'

My breath got stuck in my throat. I ran towards the rear, shoving people aside to gain a place at the railing. The rain hissed spitefully as it came down and the salt spray stung my eyes. The searchlights had lit up a broad expanse of the foaming ocean but I couln't see anything.

Then someone shouted: 'There she is. There. Over there.'

'Keep back. All passengers, please stay back.'

The sailors flung out a dozen life-savers. Some were attached to lines, others were thrown out simply to serve as flotation devices.

The sea rose and fell in massive swells and huge waves driven by the high wind buffeted the boat with a terrific violence. The vessel wallowed helplessly, swaying this way and that, utterly at the mercy of the storm.

Who would be mad enough to be out on the deck on a night like this? My stomach was tight as a tourniquet and my limbs shook uncontrollably. I wanted to jump into the water but that would have been stupid. I could barely swim and even a strong swimmer would have had a hard time in that angry sea. I just clung to the slippery rail with both hands as the deck rose and sank beneath my feet. I felt I had to be there, had to bear witness.

Soaked to the skin, I stood there shivering and blinking. The wind lashed at my jacket and all around me I could hear the shouts of people who were trying to help. Suddenly I saw the sequined headband bobbing in the boiling ocean. My blood froze in my veins and a strangled cry broke from my throat.

'No.'

I leaned over the railing as far as I could, trying to get a better look. Then I saw the headband again, floating all by itself, flashing wildly amidst the blowing spray. In the glare of the searchlights, the sequins winked and sparkled merrily. Nothing else could be seen all around, nothing, except the vast expanse of the black and bitter sea.

Molly's Choice

Dumkowski crossed the hot, sun-baked parking-lot and ducked into the cool darkness of the El Toro Bar & Grill. As he scrunched up his eyes to adjust them to the dim light, he saw her near the bar. She sat astride a stool the way a jockey sits on a racehorse. And the tall riding boots she wore over snug jeans added to the impression that she spent a lot of time around horses. She looked deeply tanned in the amber light of flame-flicker bulbs, and her sun-streaked hair hung down her back in a thick pony-tail.

Dumkowski had heard the waitresses call her Molly.

He'd seen her often in El Toro but he'd never tried to speak to her. Ted (the bartender), once told him that she owned a successful riding stable near the Sierra foothills. As suburbia expanded into farm-country, the newly-rich yuppy couples dreamed of unplugging their kids from video games and MTV and turning them into champion riders and rodeo stars. This trend kept Molly busy and brought her into town often for supplies. At least two or three times a week, Dumkowski saw her four-wheel drive, all-terrain vehicle parked in front of the restaurant.

Dumkowski did not think of El Toro as your average pick-up bar. He'd seen guys get their heads split open with cue-sticks for trying cute tactics like that. Sort of run-down and musty smelling, El Toro was the kind of place where people came to drink and watch ball games on cable TV. Dumkowski liked the joint because they served good chili con carne and a guy could eat his fill for under five bucks, beer included. It sat in a parking-lot on the edge of town, overlooking a dry arroyo cluttered with yellowish weeds, bald tires and exploded mattresses.

On Saturday nights, a rock-a-billy band amped it up for
the studly dudes who came from miles around to get tanked
and pick fights. In one corner of the dance floor sat a
mechanical bull, famous up and down the valley for
meanness. But in spite of all the folklore about cracked
skulls and mashed kidneys, the local ranch hands never
hesitated to test the steel sinews of the bull.

Molly must have sensed some kind of hunger in
Dumkowski's cautious, sidelong glances, because she turned
and fixed her frank, blue eyes on him.

'Are you a butcher?' she said.

'No,' he said, straightening up his spine, so that his elbows
were no longer resting on the bar. 'Do I look like one?'

She made a face and shook her head.

Her direct question came as a surprise, because he thought
she would never speak to him.

But now he wondered if he shouldn't take offence at
being suspected of being a butcher.

'I've had it with butchers,' she went on. 'In this town,
butchers are all you ever run into.'

She looked away and took a few more sips of wine. Then
she said: 'So what do you do for Petrini Foods?'

Once again the question irked him.

'How did you know I work there?'

'I read your aura,' she said and raised her wine-glass in a
mock salute.

'Okay,' he said. 'I fix their damn meat lockers. Or can
you see that too in my aura.'

'Hey, where's your sense of humor? Around here, if you're
not a fruit-picker or a tourist, then you've got to be working
for Petrini's. Right?'

He shrugged.

'Have another beer,' she said, 'on me. Hey, Ted, give this
guy a beer. He is not a butcher.'

Ted drew a tall one and put it on the bar. Dumkowski
took a few mouthfuls and began to see things in a brand
new light.

'I know you're Molly,' he said.

'So, you're reading auras too?' she said, and gave him a nice firm hand to shake.

'Yeah, I'm THE GREAT DUMKOWSKI, Mind Reader and Fortune Teller,' he said.

Actually, he had moved to Tracy when Petrini Foods bought up the big meat-packing plant in town. Of course, he'd wanted to stay on in San Francisco but when it came down to an ultimatum: 'move or get laid off,' he moved. Fortunately, he only had to go to the Petrini plant when something broke. This mode of working gave him a lot of free time. And because he was divorced and lived in a cramped trailer, he preferred to hang out at the El Toro, playing pool with meat-cutters, drinking beer and dreaming about getting some.

'This getting acquainted business is the shits,' Molly said.

Dunkowski nodded.

'So why don't we cut the preliminary crap,' he said, 'and do a *pas de Deux*,' he said.

'I didn't know you were into ballet.'

'I'm not,' he said. 'I'd just like to see you in a tutu.'

Suddenly, Ted leaned towards them.

'Heeee-ere come da Sheriff,' he sang out.

Dumkowski glanced back over his shoulder and saw a big man, with a blotched red face and a handlebar mustache, come in through the front door. The guy looked uncannily like the actor, Slim Pickens. His huge beer belly was pushed out in front of him and he wore a brown Smokey-the-Bear style hat on his head. He came up and stood close to Molly, breathing noisily through his mouth.

'I'd like to ask you one simple question,' he said.

'No,' said Molly, shaking her head side to side.

'I'll put it to you plainly,' said the Sheriff.

'No can do,' said Molly.

'Are you going to bail out Wiley or ain't you?' he went on in an amiable drawl as though he hadn't heard her.

'Hell, no,' said Molly. 'He can rot in jail as far as I'm concerned.'

'He thinks you oughta pony up the bail money. After all he's got a share in the ranch.'

'On paper, maybe. But he's never done shit to help out. Let him call his mother. Let her bail him out.'

'She did, remember?—the last time he got tooted up— and she almost lost her house.'

'Well, he's the fruit of her womb, isn't he. I really don't give a damn what happens to him.'

The Sheriff pushed his hat far back on his head, revealing pale shiny, skin and turned to Ted.

'Gimme one of thim Olys,' he said. 'I'm goin' off duty as of right now.'

Molly got up to leave.

'Gee, fellas, this has been swell,' she said, 'but I've got to go. And if I were you, Rex, I'd throw away the key.'

The Sheriff burped, emitting a foul gas, and wiped the foam from his mustache with the back of his left hand.

Dumkowski got off the bar-stool and followed Molly outside.

She walked to her pickup truck and got in. He stood by the door with a hand on her window ledge.

'You give rides?' he said.

'Sure,' she said. 'If you've got the money.'

'I've got the money, if you've got the time.'

'I could put you on a mild-mannered gelding for ten bucks an hour,' she said.

'I don't want a mild-mannered gelding,' he said.

'I can put you on a mare, then. If you promise to be gentle.'

'Where does True Love fit in?'

'In the barnyard, of course. Bring your own bat, though. We don't supply those.'

'I can even bring my own balls.'

'Why, that's wonderful! You're right smart for someone who's only had vocational training.'

'You're underestimating my natural gifts,' he said.

'Have you ever been on a horse before?'

'Does that matter?'

'Only if you have something against falling off.'

'I don't mind falling,' he said. 'I've fallen in love, I've fallen out of favor and I've fallen in line. I suppose I could accept falling off a horse.'

She regarded him coolly, her clear eyes fixed on his and a tiny smile at the corners of her mouth

'It's your money,' she said. 'You pay, you play.'

She started the engine and threw the truck into gear with a sudden violence.

'Come on by some time,' she said, adjusting a wide-brimmed canvas hat on her head. 'You know the way to Rancho Mirage, don't you? It's on Darien road, where it crosses Route 28.'

He nodded.

* * *

After an extra long shift at work, Dunkowski walked into the El Toro late in the afternoon. He sat at the bar and ordered the enchilada plate and a beer. 'You want the works with this?' Ted asked.

'What's that?'

'Refried beans, Spanish rice, plus taco chips with salsa.'

'Sure,' he said.

Ted wrote down his order on a tab, gave it to a waitress and placed a foaming stein before him.

'This guy, Wiley,' Dumkowski began tentatively, 'Is he Molly's husband?'

'Kinda,' Ted said, drying a glass with a white cloth. 'They're separated. She kicked his ass out on the street for being drunk on duty.'

'He sounds a bit wacko. What's he done to get the law mad?'

'I don't rightly know,' said Ted. 'But the scuttle is, he exposed himself to a bunch of high school girls. That's what the girls claim, anyway.'

'No shit?'

'Hell, I used to know girls like that,' Ted said. 'They're a pretty wild 'n' crazy bunch. In a coupla years, most of 'em'll be in Reno or Vegas, doing bump-and-grind numbers between client calls.'

'I hear ya,' said Dumkowski.

* * *

On Saturday, around sundown, Dumkowski decided to give Molly a call. The riding lessons would be over, he figured, and the horses fed and watered. Like any right-minded person, she should be sucking on a cold one by now. So he stopped at a liquor store, bought a bottle of wine and found a pay-phone.

'This is Jay,' he said. 'Jay Dumkowski.'

'So,' she said. 'What's on your mind?'

'Mashed potatoes with gravy.'

'Not on the menu today. How about baked beans?'

'I'll take 'em,' he said. 'They should go well with this Zinfandel I got at the liquor store. The guy who sold it to me, said it came from one of the best wineries in Napa.'

'Was he an oenophile?'

'Dunno. Didn't ask to see his prison record. He did have a nose-ring, though.'

'Not to worry,' she said. 'We can judge the wine ourselves.'

'Cool,' he said. 'I'm on my way.'

The one-lane road cut through green orchards of almond and walnut trees all growing in neat rows. The summer heat had dried out the wild oats growing alongside the road and turned them a pale yellow color. In the distance he could see the dull gold and tawny slopes of the hills with the inky green of pin oaks and wild lilac pushing up out of the draws and valleys. By the time he found her place, the sky had turned dark purple, and lights were coming on in the houses sitting among the orchards.

He parked under a gnarled California pepper tree, walked up to the main house and knocked. An elderly lady came to the door. She told him that Molly lived in the rooms located above the stables.

'Is she your daughter, ma'am?' he asked the old lady.

'No, we just rent this place,' she said. 'But she's almost like a daughter to me.'

Dumkowski thanked her and walked over to the stables and found the stairs that led up to the second floor. He could see the lit up windows and a strong, earthy smell of horse manure and hay filled his nose. The tread of his boots resonated loudly on the wooden steps. Molly must have heard him coming, because she opened the door before he could knock.

'Well, well, you made it,' she said, warmly. 'Supper'll be on in just a little while. You want beer or bourbon?'

'Bourbon and water'll be fine with me,' he said, and handed her the bottle of wine he'd brought.

'This should go well with the steaks,' she said, as she fixed him his bourbon and water with ice. 'Make yourself comfy. By the time I come out of the shower, it'll be time to eat.'

She disappeared into the bathroom and Dumkowski walked around the small living area, drink in hand. A couple of plain white Ginger Jar table lamps created cones of yellowish light, making it difficult for him to tell much about her taste or lifestyle. The furniture in the room looked mostly like hand-me-down Sears catalogue stuff in the Early American style. Darkness pressed against the windows and suddenly it occurred to him that Wiley could be out there, lurking among the branches of a walnut tree. He twitched his shoulders and took a big swallow from his glass.

Gradually, a warmth began to spread through his chest.

In a little while, Molly emerged from the bathroom all fresh-smelling and moist. Her blow-dried hair fell about her shoulders in a dense golden cloud and she'd wrapped herself in a flowered, silk kimono.

Dumkowski had the feeling that she wasn't wearing anything underneath the kimono.

'I thought you never took off your riding boots,' he said.

She laughed.

'I know what you mean. I think I'll die with them on.'

He helped her set the table and they sat down to eat.

'Let us partake of that Zinfandel you brought,' she said.

'Why not?' he said and poured out a glass for her.

She took a sip, rolled it around in her mouth and then swallowed the wine.

'Not bad for a young Zin from Napa,' she said. 'Though I detect a note of capriciousness on the palate that modulates into a tart audacity.'

'Where'd you learn that stuff?'

She chuckled.

'I made it up,' she said. 'Doesn't mean a thing.'

'All I want is a buzz,' said Dumkowski.

Then she said: 'Tell me about your work.'

He shook his head.

'A meat-packing plant is not the kind of topic I wanna be discussing while we eat.'

'Then tell me about your ex,' she said.

'That's easy,' he said. 'She was my high school sweetheart. Cheer-leader at Hofstetter High. Went to Beauty School...dropped out. Went to Real Estate school...dropped out. Went to Girl-Friday school...dropped out. Went to Claims Adjusting school...dropped out.'

'You're kidding?' said Molly.

'No. I'm serious,' said Dumkowski. 'Then she opened a Dog Grooming Boutique in Santa Clara. Made a profit of ten grand, after taxes and expenses, in her first year. Now she's got a chain of these Doggie Laundromats up and down the state of California, a condo in Tahoe and a house in Marin.'

'She sounds like a winner,' said Molly. 'Why did you divorce her?'

'Had to. Caught her with a man one afternoon. He was lying on his back in the middle of the living-room floor wearing nothing but a Richard Nixon mask on his face. She was sitting on his crotch—stark naked—opening and closing her mouth like a guppy.'

'Bless my niblets! Who was that masked man?'

'Lazzerone. Her accountant.'

'Hey, that's nothing. At least you didn't find her with one of her canine customers.'

'Ugh.'

'Now I suppose, I have to tell you about Wiley.'

'Only if you want to.'

'There isn't much to tell. He used be a star athlete in college. Then he got injured and took to booze. Later cocaine entered the picture. He's also got a nasty, uncontrollable temper. Not to mention some pretty bizarre sexual habits.'

'Oh, goody. Tell me about those.'

'Not at the dinner table.'

'He sounds like a real nice guy.'

'Sure. If you crossed a rabid pit-bull with a rattle snake, you'd get a Wiley.'

'Why the heck did you marry him?'

'He drove a red Corvette and liked to eat in roadside restaurants. I liked fast cars and hated to cook.'

'A match made in heaven'

'Certainly looked like one. But pretty soon the credit card bills began to pile up along with the empty liquor bottles. I could have handled that. But then Wiley discovered Peruvian Magic Dust and started getting nasty. That was more than I could take.'

'You're a survivor,' Dumkowski said.

'Fuck surviving,' she said. 'I want to be a winner, do something meaningful before they plant me in the dirt.'

'Like what?'

'I don't know,' she said. 'But I'm certainly not going to be shoveling horse dung for the rest of my life.'

'Something tells me, you won't,' he told her.

After the meal, they left the dishes on the table and moved the party into the bedroom.

She fed him a bowl of peaches floating in fresh cream.

Then she sang a duet with him.

The horses were restless in the stables below. They whinnied and stamped their hooves. The sound came up through the floorboards, like the rumble of distant thunder.

'Slow down,' she said. 'What's your hurry?'

He barely heard her. He got to thinking about the horses and suddenly started to rear and prance and paw the ground.

'Your tempo is not the same as my tempo,' he said to her.

'You can say that again,' she said.

'Your tempo is not....'

She slapped him hard across the face.

The blow stung him. Tears came into his eyes and he stumbled over some rocks and crashed into an icy stream. Everything shriveled and shrank inside him.

'I'm done,' he said. 'Now I'd like to watch TV and eat cookies.'

'Get out.' she said, hurriedly pulling on a man's shirt made of plaid flannel. 'I want you out of here. Right now.'

'My performance, I suppose, has been lackluster.'

'I've been with selfish dick-heads before,' she said, 'but you take the taco.'

'Does this mean, we won't be honey-mooning in Hawaii?' he said, poking through the bedsheets to locate his underwear.

'You've got crust,' she said.

'I coulda been a contender,' he said.

'Will you hurry?' she said. 'I have to feed the horses.'

'I can't find my underwear,' he said.

'I'll Fed-Ex it to you,' she said.

'You're a pal,' he said, but his voice lacked the note of conviction.

* * *

The really hard cases didn't start arriving at the El Toro until after ten p.m. on Saturday night, and then they came only after they'd finished the pints of Bourbon they kept in their glove compartments. The liquor numbed their brain to the point where they no longer feared the odd punch in the nose that might come their way.

Dumkowski watched these good ol' boys, with a certain amount of awe. He never could drink too much because he had a weak bladder and a bad liver. If he abused his system, he suffered.

As he walked up to the bar, he saw the back of Molly's head, the blonde pony-tail going down from beneath the white canvas hat.

Super, he thought, now I can make amends for my less than brilliant performance the other day.

'Howdy, pardner,' he said in an all-is-forgiven manner, 'What brings you here?'

Molly looked up from her wine-glass. Her eyes were watery and blood-shot. 'I'm waitin' for my wunnerfull husband,' she said. 'I hear he's out on bond.'

'Introduce me when he comes in;' Dumkowski said. 'After all, we have a lot in common.'

'I wouldn't crow if I were you,' she said. 'Wiley doesn't like competition.'

Before he could respond, the band struck up some Willy Nelson lament and everyone sank into a funk of nostalgia and liquored-up sentimentality.

'What can I get you?' said Ted.

'Shot of Bourbon with a beer chaser,' said Dumkowski.

Then he turned to Molly and said: 'Can't we be friends?'

'I don't like men as friends,' she said. 'I want a man as a lover or as an acquaintance.'

'Shit,' said Dumkowski, 'I was afraid you'd say that.'

A kind of noisy commotion at the front door made Dumkowski look back. Then he heard some guy roar: 'Outa my way, you scum-sucking toads or I'll perforate your colons with this here weapon!'

Molly said: 'I recognize the matchless braying of my True Love.'

Dumkowski looked at her as though she had lost her marbles.

A guy dressed in camouflage-pattern combat fatigues, complete with G.I. Joe boots, lumbered towards the bar. He wore a white Stetson on his head, held an Uzi in his left hand and a cigar in his right.

'Hee—eere comes Wiley,' said Ted, drawing out the name in the manner of Ed McMahon on the Johnny Carson show.

The band stopped and all the players stood looking as though they were waiting for a funeral to start. The dancers cleared the floor and faded into the walls.

Wiley walked straight up to Molly.

'I want my conjugal rights,' he said, 'and I want them now.'

Molly burst out laughing.

'This isn't Saigon, buster,' she said. 'And if I were you, I'd watch my rear.'

'Ted, you old asshole,' Wiley shouted happily, 'How've you been?'

Then he turned towards Dumkowski.

'Who are you?' he said.

His small, black eyes glittered brightly like oiled gunmetal.

Dumkowski took a step backwards, thinking hard.

'I work here,' he said.

'Then get me a martini and make it snappy,' said Wiley.

Dumkowski backed into a gaggle of waitresses behind him, his eyes fixed on the Uzi.

'You head on home, honey,' Wiley said to Molly. 'I'll be in later.'

'Just what do you think you're doing?' Molly said.

'Celebratin',' said Wiley, puffing on his cigar.

Ted set a martini on the bar and said: 'Here, Wiley. Come and get it.'

'You're all right, Tedski,' said Wiley.

He parked his cigar in an ashtray and tossed back the martini in one swift motion.

'That was good,' he said. 'Hit me again.'

'The bar is closed.' said Ted.

Wiley bit down on his cigar, bared all his teeth and began to make angry monkey faces. He was doing a lip-twitching, grimacing immitation of an angry Charleton Heston with the Uzi pointed straight at Ted across the bar.

'You think you can be persuaded to open it,' he said. 'One way or another.'

'When you put it like that,' said Ted, 'I understand.'

'Could someone call Rex and tell him to come and collect this piece of garbage,' said Molly.

'Domestic bliss is all I wanted,' said Wiley. 'Instead, I got all manner of hostility.'

He gulped down his martini and looked around with malice in his eyes.

'Gimme fifty bucks worth of quarters,' Wiley said to Ted. 'Ah'm gome tame that mean-ass bull of yours.'

Ted shot Molly a quick, inquiring glance.

She nodded.

Ted reached into a drawer under the cash register and began pulling out rolls of quarters and putting them on the bar in front of Wiley.

'Ah'm gome break the sucker's bones,' said Wiley. He scooped up all the money and put it into the pockets on the side of his pant legs.

'Watch what you're doin, Wiley,' said Ted. 'We don't have the safety mats out.'

'I don't need no safety mats,' said Wiley.

Molly shook her head and leaned back on the bar, her eyes fixed on Wiley.

Dumkowski felt a strong need to take a pee, but he knew that any move on his part might cause Wiley to react in some unpredictable way. So he stayed put.

Wiley went up to the bull and began putting quarters into the coin-box. Then he moved the dial which controlled the severity of the bucking to the half-way mark, jumped on the bull and pushed the red 'ON' button. The bull started to heave and twist violently. Wiley held on to the saddle with his left hand and kept the Uzi in his right.

'Whhooo-eeee,' he yelped. 'Waaa-aaaaa-hooo.'

By now most people had trickled out of the place, some inching towards the back-door, others out the front. They first moved slowly and cautiously towards the exits and then dashed out into the darkness outside.

'Yippppeeeee!' yelled Wiley. 'Whooo-oooo!'

The bull made a thunderous racket, as the chassis flexed and all the cams and crankshafts whirled furiously. Wiley hung on, waving the Uzi above his head.

'Call the ambulance, Ted.' Molly said, and slipped off the bar stool. 'This ass-hole's gonna need one.'

She slowly ambled up to the bull and stood near the control panel.

'This is a sissy ride,' she yelled at Wiley. 'I think you need more juice.'

She reached over and moved the intensity dial all the way to 'HIGH.'

The bull responded abruptly to the voltages coursing through its wiring. It bucked the way a real bull would react if someone shoved an electric prod up its bung-hole. It pitched and heaved and did sudden, twisting dips that threatened to rip it up from the floor.

'Whoa-aaahooo!' Wiley yelled. 'Yipppeeee!'

Those were the last sounds he uttered.

Within three quarters of a second, the bull did something that no one in El Toro had ever seen it do. It dipped, twisted, and then reared up in a lightning move that shook Wiley loose as though he were a flea and sent him flying backwards. A peculiar grimace of alarm stretched his features into an ugly mask and his arms flailed helplessly. His skull struck the protective railing which surrounded the arena. A kind of cry burst from his lungs and his neck snapped forward. The Uzi fell from his hand and he came crashing to the floor. Dumkowski knew Wiley was dead even before he hit the floor.

No one moved towards him, not even Molly. He lay still, crumpled in an awkward posture.

Molly walked back to the bar and said: 'Did you call the ambulance, Ted?'

'They're on their way,' Ted said and put a glass of white wine in front of her.

Dumkowski tried to move but for some reason he could not unglue the soles of his shoes from the floor. So he just stood there, trying hard to think of something to say to Molly. He had a hunch the band would start up pretty soon after the paramedics took away Wiley's body, and the dancers would trickle back in and the whole joint would revert to its more or less normal routines. And he also knew that he would not, after all, be asking Molly to step out on the dance floor with him. Had anyone asked him to state the reasons upon which he had based this decision, he could not have articulated them clearly. But in his heart he knew they had a lot to do with the choices Molly had made as she cantered along the paths of her destiny.

Orchek's Dire Weekend

Summers are painfully hot in Arizona. And the heat drives people crazy. As the temperature rises, people start giving you the finger at traffic-lights, tumbleweed rolls across the roads in tangled balls, parking-lots shimmer in the heat and light bounces off chromed metal and stabs your eyes.

The hot weather brings out tendencies in people, tendencies with long medical names.

Orchek had some of these tendencies. Certainly. But I still think his tribulations had more to do with the dog days of August than with his personality. Of course, there were other factors... .

He called me on Sunday morning. It was brutally hot. Rita and I were trying to recover from a breakfast of margharitas and huevos rancheros. The phone gave me a jolt.

'Leave it,' I mumbled. But Rita didn't hear me and picked up the line in the kitchen. Anymore, I can tell if it's going to be good news or bad.

'It's Orchek,' she said, covering the mouth-piece with her hand and making a face. 'I'll tell him you're out.'

'Crud. He wants me to help him move.'

'I'll say you're at the library.'

'Won't work. He knows I'm here. He needs my van to move his stuff.'

'This is the third time in one semester. Do you have to help him every time he moves?'

'Dammit! What can I do? Here, give me the phone.'

Rita said something under her breath and shoved the phone at me. She'd been on a short fuse since she'd gotten laid off from her job at the grocery store.

'Hey, Orchek, what's up?' I said, making an effort to be light and upbeat.

'Kew? What gives, man? I've been tryna reach you for hours.'

He sounded like he'd already had a few.

'We were out,' I said.

'Listen, I'm all packed up—got my stuff in boxes. Could you bring the van? Won't take but an hour or so.'

'Hmmm,' I said, 'Where's this new place?'

'1530 Yucca. You'll like it—two rooms and a backyard. It's over behind Sin City, you know, near that trailer-park.'

'Yeah, I know the area.'

This was a strip of unincorporated land that stretched alongside the bed of the Salt river. I'd spent a couple of purgatorial semesters there. The neighborhood consisted of a dozen shacks, each sitting in its own cactus-ridden patch of dust, cluttered with torn bits of paper, empty beer cans, fast-food wrappers and nameless engine parts covered in black gunk.

'Hey, you have a little house to yourself,' I told Orchek. 'Now all you need is a woman.'

'What I have is a cold six-pack looking to be done in.'

'Sounds good. We're just finishing breakfast. I'll be over soon as I can.'

'Hurry,' he said. 'I'm a mover and a shaker. Can't wait to get started.'

Why me? I moaned, as I hung up. But unable to see a way out of the dilemma, I turned to locate my sneakers.

Orchek always needed favors. Some guys are like that. Sure, he'd done me a few. He took my classes once when I started on a camping trip two days before Thanksgiving break. But I'd done more than my share for the S.O.B. He could be likeable as long as he stayed on his medication. Underneath the bright wit and wacky charm, you could see a scared little kid whose Daddy had walked off on his Mommy. And Mommy had to dump him off at Grandma's for weeks and months on end, while she struggled to make a living selling real-estate in Tucson.

His love affair with Psychology seemed nothing more than an attempt to make circus performers out of his demons. Within a year of starting Graduate school, he managed to gain considerable notoriety in the Department. He read a couple of papers full of untested theories, and quickly alienated most of the older professors. But some of the younger teachers and students considered him brilliant. He had a good chance of finishing his doctoral program on this wave of uncertainty. But his woman-trouble began to affect his work.

With women he could be Dracula and de Sade. Which is another way of saying that he was obsessive and cruel. He introduced me to most of these damsels who distressed him. He had a habit of putting them on pedestals and then systematically destroying them. No woman could or would put up with his mood-swings. Weekends usually found Orchek alone, watching some mind-numbing ball-game in DJ's and slowly getting stewed on Tequila.

But running with Orchek did have its exhilarating side. When we were together, I got the feeling that anything could happen. He reminded me of a sparkler—throwing off stars and burning fast—a sparkler lit at both ends.

When I got to Orchek's place he said: 'Here, have a beer. You look a little tense.'

'I'm OK,' I said, cracking the proffered can and tipping it back.

'I'm glad to be getting out of this stink-hole, man,' Orchek said. 'The landlord's a total jerk. He's been trying to make me pay for breaking the lock. It's all his fault that it got busted in the first place. He shouldn't have changed it without telling me. I broke the damn key tryna get in.'

'Tell him to go to hell.'

'I did. I'm not paying for all that crap.'

'Come on, let's load this shit,' I said. 'I'm eager to see the new place.'

Orchek didn't have very much in the way of possessions. Most of the heavier boxes were filled with books and papers. His clothes wouldn't have brought ten dollars at a rummage sale. All I saw in his closet were a few worn out jeans, several plaid flannel shirts, a couple of pairs of jogging shoes, and a bunch of hats in different styles.

As we carried the last blessed box out through the threshold of his apartment, the old lady who lived next door to him, opened her front door and poked out her silver head.

'Are you moving?' she asked.

'Yup,' said Orchek cheerfully.

'I'm so glad,' said the woman. 'You don't deserve to live here. In fact, you don't deserve to live…'

She slammed the door shut with a loud bang before either one of us could react.

Orchek went: 'Hyeugh, Hyeugh. She didn't care for my musical taste.'

'What musical taste?' I said.

'None o' your lip, fellah,' he snapped. 'I've already had it up to here with the geriatric thought-police.'

'Hurry,' I said, chuckling. 'Let's get out of here before she calls the cops or something.'

By the time we got all his earthly junk moved to his new place, we'd killed one twelve-pack and were looking for something to mix with the Tequila that Orchek had bought on his last visit to Nogales. He didn't have anything in the way of a blender or any margharita mix. So we ended up sipping it straight and licking salt off our thumbs, as we sat amidst the litter of over-flowing boxes and scattered clothing. Gradually the afternoon took on a hilarious quality and I lost track of time. No one had his new phone number so we felt safe, like sailors marooned on an island. I knew Rita would start getting frantic by dinner time. But I was enjoying being a fake bachelor. I decided to ride out the wave, drinking and talking man-talk with Orchek.

Round about sundown we began to think of food.
'Let's go get a pizza at the Pizza Prince,' Orchek said.
'I'll buy.'

'You better, you sonovabitch. Or I'm never helping you move again.'

So we jumped into my van and headed for the Pizza Prince. I vaguely remember shifting gears and handling the steering with exquisite caution. The old van had no shock absorbers to speak of. As it swayed and lurched around corners, I felt as though I were handling a massive space module in the zero gravity of outer space.

'Should we order a pitcher?' Orchek asked, as we sat down at a table.

'By all means,' I said, appraising a sullen, gum-chewing teen-age waitress who had ambled up.

'Whatcha guys want?' she said.

Orchek said: 'Do you have things to go?'

'Yeah,' she said, in a bored voice.

'Then get your hat and coat.'

She flashed a quick grin. 'Come on, fellas, get serious.'

Orchek said: 'OK—two pitchers. One for me and one for my friend Kew, who can shrink a head faster than you can say Sigmund Fraud.'

'No. Let's just get one,' I said. 'Later we can get another.'

'Fine. We shall do whatever Kew says,' Orchek told the waitress. 'Kew must not be thwarted or he gets testy. Isn't that right, Kew?'

The waitress smacked her gum violently and created a perfect pink bubble between her painted lips. Then she snatched the menus out of our hands and stalked off on wobbly heels.

'They'll throw us out of here,' I said to Orchek.

'Naaaah. I come here all the time. This is a second home for me.'

We snarfed up the pizza rather fast and somehow ended up back on campus with a six pack in a brown paper bag. We planned on killing the six-pack in Orchek's office.

I suppose we were both a bit drunk by now. Pretty soon Orchek had worked himself up into an irrational rage over the way he was being treated by the Psyche Department. The veins on his forehead stood out and his eyes flashed as he sputtered and spouted abuse. They were all against him because he was smarter than the whole crew of dunderheads who ran the show.

'The bastards are holding me back, I tell you,' he shouted, punching up all the buttons of the elevator. 'The diminished capacity bums don't know shit from shinola.'

'To hell with them,' I said. 'I can't wait to get out of this piss-hole.'

Soon he got to throwing books around, tearing up papers, flinging lamps and coffee apparatus to the floor. At first, it all looked hilarious and I urged him on. Laughing crazily till tears were streaming down my face, I also lobbed a book or two at the tube-lights. Imperceptibly we had moved into a mental No-Man's region of pointless violence.

I decided we had to get out of there.

'Hey, let's go to El Toro,' I said. 'It'll be full of chicks from the dorm across the street.'

That stopped him. He looked at me wild-eyed and excited: 'Far out, Kew. You are man of vision. Let's go.'

As we stepped out into central corridor to get to the elevators, Orchek took a running leap and swung a fist against a big schoolroom clock which stood out at a right angle from the wall. The glass shattered with a loud crack and rained all around us. The minute hand got twisted and the clock stopped at 8:35.

'Ouch!' he yelped. His hand started to bleed from several deep cuts.

'Damn you. Look what you've done?' I said.

'Screw 'em all ,' he shouted.

'Let's get out of here,' I said, 'before someone sees us.'

Half pulling, half dragging him, I got us out of the building and into the van. I wrapped his hand in an old shirt while he squealed in pain. But by the time I drove into the parking lot of El Toro, he was giggling happily once again.

'Now Time stands still in the Psyche Department,' I told Orchek.

'Hey, Time has always stood still in that stupid shit pit,' he responded. 'But now, at least, they'll be able to see it.'

We bellied up to the El Toro bar in high spirits.

'I'll buy,' I said.

'No,' said Orchek, 'I'll buy.'

'No, no, you bought the pizza.'

I got us a round of margharitas and checked out the place. El Toro had the reputation of being a pick-up bar. The clientele consisted of secretaries and insurance adjusters in cheap hair pieces, who came to prey on them. This crowd drank massive fruit-drinks with umbrellas in them. Rougher types usually occupied the bar stools. These were guys who had vending-machine routes and tattooed forearms. They had high hopes of scaring up some undergrad tail. But pairing up remained problematical. The men often drank too much, turned nasty, and ended up puking their guts out in the Oleander bushes behind the restaurant.

Orchek and I finished our drinks rather swiftly and ordered a second round. I was sitting facing the front door, chewing on a swizzle stick. So when Lana walked in, she caught my eye right away. But I didn't say anything. I was hoping Orchek wouldn't see her. He'd been dating her off and on for a couple of months, in his usual lackadaisical fashion. It had been a turbulent and erratic relationship and made no sense to me. Nor did Orchek have a clue. When he was with Lana, they could go from tender cooing and billing to vicious screaming matches with alarming swiftness.

Lana had come in with a thickly-muscled, blonde fellow in red Bermuda shorts, a flowered Hawaiian shirt and rubber thongs—a nice, healthy, surfer-boy.

Orchek caught sight of them in the mirror above the bar and whirled around on his stool.

A sudden in-rush of blood made his face red. Lana locked eyes with us for a split second and then quickly turned towards her companion who seemed to be scanning the restaurant area for a free table.

I put my hand on Orchek's arm.

'Stay put,' I snarled.

Soon the hostess hustled forward and led Lana and her be-flowered escort to a table on the far side of the restaurant, hidden from our view by a screen of ferns.

'Who's she with?' I asked Orchek.

'Dunno,' he said.

'Could be her brother,' I said.

'Yeah, sure,' he said. 'And I could be Burt Lancaster.'

'Easy now. Just leave her alone.'

'Maybe I should go over and say hi.'

'Maybe you shouldn't.'

'I don't think she saw me.'

'She didn't.'

Suddenly, he got up. I grabbed his shoulder.

'Hey, I'm just going to the toilet, OK?'

He flashed a lop-sided grin at me and then ambled away beyond the screen of plants. I took a few nervous sips of my drink and looked at my watch. It said 9:30, but it felt much later. Fatigue and booze were catching up with me.

I sat there in a kind of fog, thinking fuzzily about the scene I'd face when I got home. Rita would do her bitch-kitty number undoubtedly, angling for a rip-roaring fight. At times like this, I hated being married. As I sat there brooding over my lot in life, I lost track of time. Orchek seemed to be taking a long time for some reason. Then it occurred to me that he could be getting sick in the toilet. I wondered if I should go and check up on him.

Just as I stood up on wobbly legs, I heard loud, angry voices coming from beyond the screen of plants. Orchek's was the loudest, rising shrill and drunk above all the other voices.

I had no desire to get involved in a three-way lovers war. Yet, I felt a certain obligation to extricate Orchek from the situation, keep him from making an utter fool of himself in front of a lot of people. But even as I stood there debating, the whole thing escalated into a regular brawl. The sounds of crashing tables and breaking china indicated that Orchek and the other guy were resorting to cave-man tactics. The bartender, a body-builder type himself, reacted fast. He cleared the bar in a leap and raced forward to separate the combatants. By now a lot of other people were also converging on the scene.

But the fracas ended in a matter of minutes. The burly bartender came up behind Orchek and caught him in a half-Nelson. Orchek struggled to get loose, but couldn't. His nose bled profusely and the gore covered the front of his T-shirt. The other guy appeared to be undamaged. He stood by the far window, calm but flushed. The bartender and I pushed and shoved Orchek into the Men's toilet. I filled up a sink with cold water and pushed his head down. He was still acting pretty wildly and tried to get away from us.

'I'll kill the fucking bastard,' he hissed. 'I'll kill him. Lemme go.'

'Calm down, ass-hole. I told you not to go near her.'

After a while he calmed down. I dragged him out to the parking lot, talking to him all the while, trying to make him see the futility of his behavior. I finally got him into the van and started to pull out. He made a sudden movement and jumped out of the moving vehicle. I jammed on the breaks, ran after him and brought him down with a flying tackle.

'You get your sorry ass in that van, or I'll kick your butt into next week,' I told him. 'You'll get yourself killed.'

When we got back to his place, I made some coffee for him.

'You don't own Lana. She's free, white and twenty-one. She can do what she damn well pleases.'

'She's a rotten, two-timing bitch, is what she is,' said Orchek.

'You better forget about her. OK?' I told him. 'That's my advice to you as a friend.'

He nodded morosely, pressing a wet towel to his nose.

'See you later,' I said. 'I've gotta go.'

Rita was fast asleep. She murmured something foul as I crawled into bed but was too sleepy to start a fight. I lay on my back for a while and stared at the ceiling. The room seemed to be going round and round.

Again, it was the shrill scream of the phone that woke me up. It sounded bad: insistent, relentless.

'Will you get that goddamn phone,' Rita shouted finally. 'I'm sure it's for you.'

I reached over and grabbed the phone.

'Mmm-yellow,' I said.

I heard a hoarse whisper.

'Kew, it's me. Orchek.'

'God, Orchek. It's four in the morning. What's going on?'

'Kew, I need you, man. Could you come over? I'm serious. Something terrible has happened.'

His voice shook as he spoke.

'What are you talking about?'

'Lana...'

'Lana? What's she doing at your place? How did she know where....'

'Rick told her where I lived. Remember him? The body-builder—he tends bar at El Toro. I'd mentioned my new place to him.'

'But why...?'

'I don't know. I guess she wanted to talk...after what happened.'

'Is she OK?'

'No. I don't think so. I mean, it's a mess, man. She's bleeding all over. We got into fight. It's bad, Kew. Please, please, could you come over? I need you, man.'

Suddenly my bones began to shiver and I was very wide awake.

'Stay right there,' I told him. 'I'm on my way.'

'What's going on?' Rita mumbled sleepily.

'I don't quite know,' I said, slipping into my jeans and grabbing the keys. 'Lana and Orchek had a fight or something. I think she's hurt.'

Rita uttered a muffled obscenity.

'Has anyone called an ambulance?' she asked.

'I don't think so.'

'You better,' she said in a tone of warning.

I quickly dialed the emergency number and explained where Orchek lived. 'Get there quickly as you can,' I begged.

I jumped into the van and drove out to Orchek's neighborhood as fast as I could. My eyes burned as though they had been raked with hedgehogs and my head was gonging with pain. When I pulled up in front of his place, I doused my lights and looked and listened cautiously. Orchek's house was dark. A dog yipped in someone's backyard and a lone coyote howled in response.

I walked up to his door.

'Hey, Orchek,' I said in a hoarse whisper. 'It's me.'

I twisted the knob and went in.

'Turn on some lights, man,' I told him.

'Can't,' I heard him say. 'They haven't hooked up the power yet.'

'Shit!' I muttered. 'Where's Lana?'

'In the kitchen,' said Orchek. 'She's hurt bad, Kew.'

'I called 911. The ambulance should be here any second.'

'Oh, God!,' he moaned.

I lit a match and walked towards the kitchen.

'Lana,' I called urgently, 'Lana.'

I heard a low, muffled gurgle. In the fluttering glare of the match, I saw her sitting on the floor, her back propped up against the refrigerator. She was holding on to a knife handle which protruded just below her right clavicle. There was blood all over the tiled floor and her eyes were locked in an unseeing stare.

'Holy Christ!' I muttered, stepping back. 'What the hell did you do, Orchek?'

Then the match went out, and we were in utter darkness.

The Woman in the Black Veil

A terse telegram: 'Doctor Sahib injured. Car accident. Come immediately.' I don't remember who sent it, but it had come from Sialkot. So much time, so many years have gone by. I wonder if it even had a sender's name. I was only nine or ten years old at the time, and my brain got very muddled with anxiety.

I'd been playing with some neighborhood boys in the unpaved street in front of our house on Humayun Street with its single, half-dead eucalyptus tree. It was getting late and the chilly, gray winter afternoon had darkened to a smoke-blue evening. Suddenly, I noticed a courier getting off his bicycle in front of our house. My mother was attending classes at her college, so I took the envelope from the man and broke the seal.

It did not take me long to decide that I had to get the news to her right away. So I pulled out my bike, and pedaled as fast as I could towards her college. After running up and down around several empty corridors, I finally found her classroom and handed her the telegram. She became very pale and, for a second, I thought she might faint. But she didn't. While the other students looked on, sort of amazed, she spoke briefly to her professor and we hurried home in a horse carriage. She explained what had happened to our old Ayah, who functioned as our cook and maid, stuffed a few clothes and toiletries into a suitcase and we rushed out of the house again.

Then she did something totally unexpected and extravagant. Instead of heading for the train station or the bus depot, we headed straight for an automobile rental agency where she hired a car and driver to take us to Sialkot.

I knew this would cost us a lot of money. Sialkot was nearly a hundred miles away.

'We have to get there as quickly as possible,' she said.

I had never seen her act so boldly, or be so eager to get to Sialkot. Her relationship with my father had, more or less, withered away over the last few years. In fact, we had moved to Lahore from Sialkot several years earlier, when she grew tired of the way he treated her.

As the car carried us smoothly and speedily through a darkening landscape, I started to think of all the events which had forced my mother to move to Lahore. And in these jumbled and confusing reveries, the image of the woman in the black veil was always there, hovering and floating in the background like an evil thing, something I feared, something that had come into our lives many years earlier, when I was just a child...

* * *

Mummy always feels soft when I hug her. Daddy's cheeks scratch my face and make it itch.

'Who will you marry when you grow up?' Auntie Sarwat says.

'I will marry Mummy,' I say.

'You silly boy,' says Auntie Sarwat, laughing. 'No, you won't. You will marry your cousin, Fawzia.'

I beg Mummy for a rabbit and Mummy gets me a rabbit. But the rabbit wiggles and wiggles and tries to run away. So I squeeze it with my hands. And then I feel the rabbit's bones under the fur. Then I put it back in its cage.

'Be gentle,' Mummy says. 'Don't hurt the poor thing.'

'Yes, Mummy,' I say.

Mummy says, 'Be careful. Don't walk off with a stranger.'

Mummy says, 'Bad people steal children and force them to beg.'

I say, 'I don't like bad people.'

Mummy says, 'Don't open the door till you know who it is.'

But I open the door, when I hear the knock. And this woman covered up with a long veil made of black cloth is standing there. I don't know who she is. Her face is hidden behind a curtain of black gauze.

'Is Doctor Sahib in?' she asks.

No, I say, Daddy is not back from the clinic.

She stands there very still and silent. The black veil or 'burka' covers her from the top of her head to her ankles. I wonder what she wants. But I do not say anything. I wonder if she will grab me and turn me into a beggar boy.

'But Mummy is home,' I say in an overly loud voice. 'I'll go tell her.'

I turn on my toes and race back towards the kitchen.

'What is it?' Mummy asks.

'There's a woman in a black burka at the door and she wants to see you.'

'Show her into the sitting room,' Mummy says. 'I'll be there in a few minutes.'

But when I get back to the front door, the woman isn't there. She seems to have disappeared.

I close the door, hook the latch, and return to the kitchen.

'The woman's vanished,' I say.

Mummy has a knife in one hand and a potato in the other.

'Don't make up stories,' Mummy says.

'I'm not,' I say. 'Please bury a potato in hot ashes for me.'

'Must have been a patient,' Mummy says. 'Probably decided to go to the clinic.'

She buries a potato in hot ashes for me. I love to eat potatoes baked in hot ashes with lemon juice and salt and black pepper on them. So I sit down near the fire and push sticks into the flames and wait.

* * *

My father was a doctor, the best and busiest one in Sialkot, and spent all day at his clinic. He made lots and lots of money and we lived in a large bungalow with a verandah and a garden all around. Sick people came to his clinic from all the villages around Sialkot. They liked Daddy and said they had faith in him. He had a jolly, friendly way of talking to people and even the sickest person cheered up in his presence.

Daddy's clinic was on Rasheed Street and I loved going there. He rented several rooms on the ground floor of a building and as soon as you walked in, you noticed the strange and interesting smells. The smells came from a tiny room in the back called the 'Dispensary' which was filled with all sorts of colored liquids in huge jars and bottles. His assistant used to crush pills and mix powders in this dispensary. I got to know the names and colors of many medicines: Tincture of Iodine was yellow and had a sharp odor. Mercurochrome was red and you used it on minor bruises. I also knew the sweet taste of Glycerin because my tonsils had been painted with it many times for coughs and throat infections. Cod Liver Oil smelled like dead fish and had a horrible taste. Carminative mixture had a spicy flavor and was good for your tummy. Best of all were the nose-burning odors of disinfectant and methylated spirits.

It was a busy place, my father's clinic, and people came to visit him even when they weren't sick. He had lots of friends. And they would sit around chatting with him for hours. Still he managed to see enough patients to keep up his extravagant style of living. We even owned a car—a white Morris Minor—and Daddy used to drive around town in it as fast as he could, dodging goats and bullock carts laden with vegetables.

Daddy—I used to call him Abba-ji—looked huge to me in those days, when my eyes were at the level of his knees. He was tall and big-boned and had a large belly and a high, wide forehead. He loved to eat rice and curried chicken and shami kebabs and carrot halva. His appetite was always good

and I don't think he was sick even for a day in his life. He
had a cheerful attitude and enjoyed everything he did. I
think he even enjoyed the fights he had with my mother.

When he walked down the old bazaar of Sialkot, people
rushed up to him, grabbed him by the arm and asked his
advice on all kinds of problems. Whether it was a rash that
wouldn't go away, or a daughter who needed a husband
and a dowry, Dr Sahib always had an answer. Neighborhood
children wrapped themselves around his legs and would not
let go until he gave them the sweet-and-sour throat lozenges
he always carried in his pocket.

But there was another side to my father...

* * *

The night is cold and it is very late. I am burrowed deep
under the quilt in my mother's bed. She is sitting on the
edge, but I can feel her warmth. She is crying, and my
father is walking about the room, growling and barking at
her.

I wish he would stop. He's been tormenting her for hours.
I wish I were somewhere else—somewhere far away. I wish
he would be quiet.

'I'll leave,' my mother says between sobs. 'I'll take Junaid
and go to Lahore.'

'Go!' he yells. 'Go now. Go tonight. See if I care. I want
you out of this house.'

I sink deeper under the quilt and put my hands over my
ears. I hate their endless quarrels. They've been arguing all
evening, my father swearing and cursing, and calling her
every foul name he can think of. My mother fights back,
accuses him of all kinds of sins. But she's no match for him.
He can bully her with ease.

She brings up his meetings with female patients. She
knows why these women come to see him. They are not
really sick. He shrugs. He has no shame or remorse. When

she mentions her brother and says he is a good husband, Abba-ji makes fun of him. Calls him a shriveled up carrot.

By now she is weeping uncontrollably, overwhelmed by his nasty rudeness.

I crawl out from under my warm tunnel and put an arm around my mother's neck.

'Don't cry, Mummy,' I say to her. 'Please don't cry.'

I can barely hold back my own tears.

When my mother got angry at Daddy, she always said she would leave him and go to Lahore. She never really meant it, I think. But after he beat her up badly with a cane, she decided the time had come to leave. I saw those long, red marks on her skin. She lifted her chemise and showed them to me.

'Your father did this,' she said, crying without making a sound. 'I can't live with him anymore.'

'I'll go with you, Mummy,' I said bravely, but my heart was sinking into my sandals.

I put my arms around her and buried my face in her bosom.

The rickety wagon of our life was rushing down a steep slope towards the edge of a cliff. We would never be able to get off this wagon. We were headed for a crash —a disaster. And, somehow, in this endless nightmare, I always saw the woman in the black veil floating in the background—watching, waiting...

* * *

My mother is not home. I think she has gone to see Auntie Sarwat in Lahore. I wanted to go with her but I had school. Mother said she was only going for a few days and would be back soon. I hated being left behind, even though the trip was not really a social visit. My mother wanted to talk about serious matters with Auntie Sarwat.

When I get back from school, I go into the kitchen in search of something to eat. There is no one in the kitchen.

Daddy had told the cook to take the afternoon off and go and visit her family. So I pour out a glass of milk for myself and get a piece of bread. The house feels very empty and silent. It is a hot afternoon and a crow is sitting on the ledge outside the kitchen. He keeps cawing and cawing. The old cook told me that when you see a crow sitting on a wall cawing like this, it is a sign that we will have visitors. I didn't really believe her, but the very next minute the crow proves her right. The front door opens suddenly and Daddy comes in. This surprises me, because he never comes back from the clinic in the afternoon.

There is a woman with him. She is covered in a black veil.

'The poor thing is very sick,' Daddy says to me. 'I'm going to examine her in the sitting room. Go and play in the verandah and don't make too much noise.'

I nod my head.

He leads the woman into the sitting room and shuts the door behind him and bolts it.

I am all by myself and can do as I like. So I decide to peek through the keyhole. Daddy has forgotten about the keyhole. Or he doesn't think I will peek. But I want to know everything.

I can only see a small area directly in front. The back of a chair cuts off the lower part of the room and half the long couch. The woman in black is lying on the couch. She looks tired. I can see Daddy's hands, as he examines her, pressing here and there and pulling and tugging at her clothes. Eventually, I see the pale slope of her tummy and my father's face close to her skin. He seems to be listening. Then he kneels at the edge of the couch and all I can see is his broad back. The woman starts to cry and moan as though she is in pain.

She really is sick, I think. I can see her face. It is very pale. And at one point her chemise gets pushed way up and her breasts spill out. My father holds her narrow waist in both hands and pulls her half off the couch. She raises a hand to her mouth and seems to be biting her knuckles. Then I see

his white-shirted back again, moving over her and her
shoulders jerking up and down. The room is dimly lit and
everything seems small and blurred through the keyhole.

Finally, I get tired of standing with my eye pressed to the
door. So I go and get a tennis ball and start to bounce it
against a wall.

That's when the cook comes back.

'Daddy's home,' I tell her. 'He is seeing a patient.'

'Then keep the noise down, son,' the cook tells me.

After a while Daddy opens the living-room door and
comes out. He doesn't say anything to me but goes straight
towards the bathroom. I hear him in there washing his
hands. Later, when the old cook sees Daddy leading the
woman out of the house, she shakes her head and mutters
something under her breath which I do not understand.

* * *

There is much that I do not understand. There are so many
paradoxes, so many contradictions. This is the main reason
why I grew up so stupid, so confused.

Even though Daddy was absent from our life in Lahore,
he became a bigger and bigger presence in my mental
universe as I got older. My mind has always been like a
huge whispering gallery in which echoes and images clash
and collide without making any sense.

At first, I sided with my mother and joined her in
despising my father. But later, as my own sex hunger woke
up, I started to understand his desperation. I also realized
that I had the same streak of cruelty that he had.

I've been to many psychologists and psychoanalysts. But
no one has been able to help me. I am sure there is a
connection between the events that took place when I was a
child and my current sexual problems. There is a connection
between certain memories and images and my feelings
towards women. And when I encircle a woman's waist with
my arm, something makes it impossible for me to go on.

Perhaps there is a connection between my failure as a man and that incident with the rabbit...

* * *

The afternoon is very still and hot and I am alone in the house. The air is not moving. The leaves of the peepul trees in the front yard seem dead. A hollow silence fills every room of the house. Bored and restless, I go to the rabbit's cage and pull it out. The cage has a very bad odor. The smell of urine is everywhere. The rabbit has made it very dirty. I try to hold the rabbit in my lap but he keeps wriggling, wanting to get away. The rabbit's thin bones feel like sticks through the covering of skin and fur. I hold it more tightly, but that makes him jerk even harder. In frustration, I put the rabbit back in his cage.

Suddenly, I want to do something I've never done before. I decide to drown the rabbit in water as a sort of punishment. A thrill of excitement goes down my spine. I get a tin bucket and take it to the hand-pump, just outside the kitchen door. I find it hard to pump the water. But I place all my weight on the long, metal handle. This makes it come down and a thin trickle of water comes out of the spout. I jump on the handle again and again, getting very winded with the effort I am making. Slowly the bucket starts to fill up. By now I am sweating and panting. When the bucket is about half full, I carry it to the rabbit's cage, half dragging, half carrying it between my legs.

I open the cage door, grab the rabbit by the neck and pull him out. He jerks his hind legs as I hold him above the bucket. Then I grab him with both hands and shove him down into the bucket. The rabbit struggles and kicks, but I push his head under the water. He starts to thrash around even more wildly, but I keep pushing him down. I can feel his limbs twitching and jerking. This goes on for several minutes. Then suddenly, I can't stand this any more. My heart is beating very fast and my face feels hot with pulsing blood. I pull him up again. The rabbit blinks his ruby red eyes rapidly. He looks small and skinny as a rat, with his wet fur sticking to his skin. I am suddenly overwhelmed by a sense of disgust and shame. I put the rabbit back in his cage and kick the bucket over. I go and sit in the verandah. I can see the mynah birds looking for food under the peepal trees. The sun is still high in the sky but I feel as though I have a block of ice inside my stomach.

* * *

My mother had always been rather a plump person and as she got older, she became quite big. I don't think she ate more food than anyone else. It was just the way her system was. I saw her naked once. She had rolls of skin and folds of flesh that tumbled down her body. She also had a huge scar that ran up and down her entire left side.

One day, when she was still a very young girl, she was sitting near a pan of milk that was boiling away on top of a charcoal stove. Someone knocked the pan over by accident and the milk fell all over her left side. She got terrible burns and almost died. Over time, the burns healed, but the scar proved permanent. I was shocked when I saw that scar for the first time and never forgot what it looked like. It looked like the African continent.

For my mother, the body was not very important. Only the brain mattered. But I am beginning to think that there was a connection between this scar on her body and the way my father treated her. He too must have been shocked when he saw it for the first time on his wedding night. I think her marriage began and ended on her wedding night. He never forgave her for this physical flaw. And even though he was not the type who could have been a loyal and faithful husband, the scar on her body made it easy for him to turn to other women.

His tirades and temper tantrums became daily events and made her life miserable. This went on for years until she was half crazy with despair. Finally, she hit upon a clever idea. She told my father she would set up house in Lahore so that I could attend a better school. Sialkot was a small town and did not have good schools. Abba-ji welcomed the idea. He immediately saw it as a way of getting her out of his life, without making the entire family angry at him. He promised to send money to support us, but that was a lie...

At first, I hated our life in Lahore. We rented two tiny, bare rooms in a shabby section of town, close to a huge graveyard. This was the best my mother could afford on her schoolteacher's salary. We owned a couple of rickety chairs, a couple of string cots, some pots and pans and a few books. And we had no means of transportation of our own, such as a horse carriage or a motor car. Nevertheless, living in this poverty-stricken, ugly way did not upset my mother. For the first time in her life she was quite free to pursue her own goals. She was free to learn, free to go about as she pleased. Moreover, her heart and mind were full of the wealth of great literature and she lived entirely in her mind, in a world filled with grand images and ideas.

But the awareness that we were no longer living like rich people made me quite miserable. I became very shy and nervous and hated meeting people, especially relatives.

Once in a great while, Daddy sent us a little cash via telegraphic money order. And my mother bought some necessities. But the shortage of money was a constant in our lives. We were no longer a part of Abba-ji's world. And even though I never admitted this in front of my mother, I missed Sialkot. I missed the hustle and bustle of the clinic. I missed the bungalow with its green lawn and red bougainvillea bending over the verandah. I missed the big, jolly presence of my father. Of course, when summer came around and my school closed down for three months, I was permitted to go to Sialkot. And summer after summer that bungalow revealed to me secrets and sensations that completed my transformation from boy to man. The house contained odors that stung all my nerves into a state of tense wakefulness.

The women who came to see my father left the stains of their presence on the couches and cushions in the living-room. Their perfumes lingered behind long after they had left. The peculiar smells of their diseases and open wounds permeated the very walls of that house. Summer after summer these odors drove me into self-tormenting frenzies and I would lock myself in the bathroom for hours. I would stay there and hold myself tightly until everything melted before my eyes and my knees buckled. I discovered the joys and torment of the flesh in that house in Sialkot.

My mother was so noble, so high-minded, so bright and yet, for some strange reason, I started to hate her as I got older. There is no logical explanation for why I felt this way. The poor thing did everything in her power to make life easier for us. She realized that she needed more education and started attending a local college. She also kept on teaching, mainly because we needed the money and also because she did not want to be dependent on my father. She wanted to make a life of her own. Perhaps this is why I resented her. I blamed her for our break with Sialkot. Lahore could never be Sialkot. In Sialkot we had lived a gracious, upper-class life with our motor-car and bungalow. In Lahore we were reduced to scrounging and scrimping alongside the lower classes. There was no lawn and flower-festooned verandah in Lahore, no motor car, no dinner parties, no visits to the Civil Lines Club.

But as the years went by, I felt a change coming over me. Sialkot ceased to be important and the focus of my mind and my imagination shifted to Lahore. My attitude towards Lahore changed as I began to build my own life, my own circle of friends, my own links with the city's parks and public places. As I got a little older, I began to appreciate the advantages of living there. Lahore had many excellent schools and colleges, and famous Moghul monuments and public gardens. We also had quite a few relatives in various quarters of the city. Some of our relatives lived in grand bungalows surrounded by trees and flowers; others occupied ancient, crumbling houses inside the walls of the Old City with its narrow streets and evil odors. But they all made my mother feel welcome. They admired her great learning, her courage and her independent spirit.

With the passage of years, I started to like the crowded, colorful bazaars of Lahore where I could linger as long as I liked with my head full of dreams. I became a part of the current of life that flowed through these streets. Lahore became my city.

* * *

We covered more than a hundred miles in a little over two hours. Still, by the time we reached the Civil Hospital in Sialkot it was very late. Mummy paid the driver one hundred Rupees. I had never seen a hundred rupee banknote in my life before.

A nurse led us quickly to the private quarters where they had placed my father. My heart fluttered in my chest when we entered his room. Abba-ji lay covered in white bed-sheets, breathing through a rubber tube. He had suffered a lot of injuries: a fractured forehead, a broken jaw, a cracked leg, a shattered ankle, torn ribs, and there was some talk that he might have punctured a lung. They had wrapped his head and chest tightly in bandages and a plaster cast covered his left leg. The doctor standing near him, shook his head grimly. It would be a miracle if he pulled through. It was a miracle that he was still alive. My father was tough, the doctor said. Anyone else would have died, considering all the loss of blood and all the damage that had been done to the body.

They had given him painkillers and sedatives to keep him calm. But when Mummy and I entered the room, he noticed us. His eyes were like clots of blood. I went up and touched his cheek timidly.

Mummy pulled me back gently.

'You go and get something to eat,' she said.

I felt grateful towards her for letting me escape. In another minute, I would have burst into tears. Seeing him lying there, bleeding and broken and helpless, gave me a terrible jolt. I realized suddenly how much I loved him and how much he meant to me. I forgot all about his temper tantrums and his selfishness. I just wanted him to live, to pull through. I did not know how close he was to dying.

The old cook caressed my head and put her arm around me. She led me to an adjacent room which had been set up as a temporary kitchen with a kerosene stove and a few pots and pans. She fed me some warmed up rice with lentils and made up a cot for me in a corner. I fell into an uneasy sleep.

That night I saw the woman in the black veil again. She came into the room where my father lay, and stood at his feet. I got the feeling that she was waiting for something.

I woke up with a start, sweating and breathing hard. With my pulse throbbing madly, I tiptoed into Daddy's room. I could hear him inhaling and exhaling noisily. Mother sat near him in a circle of light reading the poems of Hafiz.

'What's the matter, son?' she asked.

'Nothing,' I said.

'Go back to bed, ' she said. 'Don't worry. I'm watching over him.'

I shuffled back to bed, but I couldn't sleep for a long time. I was afraid of the woman in the black veil who haunted my dreams. I had a feeling she was still there, waiting for me in that gray zone where this world fades away into the world of dreams, where the things we desire and the things we dread are often the same.